THE ADVENTURES OF
MR. NICHOLAS WISDOM

THE ADVENTURES OF
MR. NICHOLAS WISDOM

Ignacy Krasicki

Translated by
Thomas H. Hoisington

With an Introduction by
Helena Goscilo

Northwestern University Press
Evanston, Illinois

Northwestern University Press
Evanston, Illinois 60201-2807

First published in Polish as *Mikołaja Doświadczyńskiego Przypadki* by Zakład Narodowy Imienia Ossolińskich—Wydawnictwo, 1921. English translation copyright © 1992 by Northwestern University Press. Introduction copyright © 1992 by Northwestern University Press. All rights reserved.

Published 1992

Printed in the United States of America

ISBN: cloth 0-8101-1014-8
        paper 0-8101-1039-3

Library of Congress Cataloging-in-Publication Data

Krasicki, Ignacy, 1735–1801.
  [Mikołaja Doświadczyńskiego przypadki. English]
  The adventures of Mr. Nicholas Wisdom / Ignacy Krasicki;
translated by Thomas H. Hoisington; with introduction by Helena Goscilo.
      p. cm.
  Translation of: Mikołaja Doświadczyńskiego przypadki
  ISBN 0-8101-1014-8 (lib. bdg.). – ISBN 0-8101-1039-3 (pbk.)
  I. Title.   II. Title: Adventures of Mister Nicholas Wisdom.
PG7157.K7M513   1992
891.8'535—dc20   91-42474
                                                               CIP

The paper used in this publication meets the minimum requirements of American National Standard for Information Sciences—Permanence of Paper for Printed Library Materials, ANSI Z39.48-1984.

Contents

Acknowledgments

The translation of Krasicki's novel would not have been possible without the help of friends and family. I am particularly grateful to Paulina Lewin of the Ukrainian Research Center of Harvard University, who painstakingly checked my translation for accuracy and patiently explained to me passages of the Polish text difficult to comprehend, and to my wife and colleague, Sona Hoisington, whose encouragement as well as editorial interventions made the final version possible. I would also like to express my gratitude to Helena Goscilo of the University of Pittsburgh, who, in addition to composing the informative introduction to this volume, improved the readability of the text, editing it in its entirety, and to Curtisteen Steward, who typed a large part of the manuscript so well and so quickly.

The preparation of this translation was made possible in part by a grant from the Division of Research Programs of the National Endowment for the Humanities, an independent federal agency.

Introduction

*Virtus est vitium fugere, et sapienta prima
Stultitia caruisse.
(To flee vice is the beginning of virtue, and the beginning of
wisdom is to have got rid of folly.)*

Horace, *Epistles*

Poland during the Enlightenment

Ignacy Krasicki (1735–1801) stands unchallenged as the preeminent man of letters during the Polish Enlightenment. A worldly, multifaceted figure of formidable erudition and unflagging vitality, he made his mark as an administrator, royal adviser, clergyman, and publicist at a particularly turbulent stage in Poland's beleaguered history. The cultural ferment in Poland during the second half of the eighteenth century could not avert or contain the political chaos that eventually culminated in the three Partitions (1773, 1793, 1795), erasing an independent Poland from the map of Europe. Poland's internal problems indisputably facilitated its gradual piecemeal annexation by neighboring Russia, Austria, and Prussia. By midcentury, the country that the late Renaissance had reputed as a citadel of cosmopolitanism, intellectual energy, and religious tolerance resembled little more than a quagmire littered with the debris of medieval customs and thought. This precipitate decline may be ascribed to several factors: Poland's lack of dynastic continuity; the nobility's control of the throne, as well as their provincialism, hostility to all innovation, and terminal self-interest (all traits of "Sarmatism"); an abortive legislative process paralyzed by the right of *liberum veto;* and a prepotent Church with a virtual monopoly on both publishing and education. Under an oligarchy of magnates (e.g., the Radziwiłł, Czartoryski, and Zamojski families), power was concentrated in the hands of a privileged few intent solely on wielding it for their own profit, to extend their dominion or augment their already fabulous wealth. The depotentiated Saxon monarchs who (mis)ruled Poland from 1697 until 1763 seemed indifferent to the drastic need for political and social reform: specifically, for the consolidation of royal authority, the abolition of the *liberum veto* in favor of a parliament operating by majority rule, a fundamental revision of the outmoded constitution, a decrease in the nobility's arbitrary freedoms, a modernization of education, and a more lively interaction with progressive factions in Europe.

With the election of Catherine II's protégé Stanisław Augustus Poniatowski to the Polish throne in 1764, the country entered its Stanislavian (or Augustan) period of enlightened reform and cultural revival. Although the Commonwealth of Poland-Lithuania irretrievably lost not only its active role in the international arena but also, eventually, its status as an independent nation, Poniatowski's reign nonetheless was a time of intense struggle for Poland's independence, of moral regeneration, and of remarkable achievements on multiple fronts. The country's devastating political losses did not hamper the intellectual and artistic gains enabled largely by the initiative of its sophisticated, forward-looking monarch. A controversial personality with conflicting allegiances that undermined his foreign policy, Poniatowski in his role of Maecenas implemented a series of innovations that wrested Poland from its retrogressive traditions and partially restored its former cultural standing in Europe.

The wheels of change actually had started rolling a few decades earlier, owing to the efforts of foreign visitors who settled in Poland, such as the German printer Mitzler de Kolof and his countryman Michael Gröll (Krasicki's future publisher), and of those Polish nobles whose travels abroad facilitated links with cultural centers throughout France, England, Italy, and Germany. Under the impact of imported ideas, Poland revised its educational system and introduced institutions calculated to stimulate the cultural development of an intellectually apathetic population. Accordingly, 1741 witnessed the founding in Warsaw of the Collegium Nobilium, where physical sciences, the philosophy of Locke and Wolff, and the works of Voltaire and Molière supplemented the outmoded classics curriculum for young noblemen. Six years later a sizable public library opened in Warsaw. In the early 1750s the Jesuit schools that had degenerated into a training ground for flowery rhetoric in Latin and Polish underwent substantive revamping. Partly to combat obscurantism through "artistic instruction," they now incorporated theater and literature into their programs (e.g., the school plays of the Jesuit playwright and educator Franciszek Bohomolec).

Attuned to the profound transformations sweeping over Western Europe in the wake of a new philosophy, Poniatowski recognized the importance of secularizing education, improving the economy, and promoting science. His accession to the throne accelerated the pace of wide-ranging measures designed to bring Polish thinking more into line with contemporary European thought. A national public theater opened in Warsaw (1765), its main purpose the inculcation of progressive social and political values and of conduct guided by the twin principles of reason and moderation. The same year saw the appearance of the *Monitor*. Moralistic in orientation and committed to "new ideas," it was the first periodical in Poland modeled on Addison and Steele's *Spectator*. The first exclusively literary journal, *Pleasant and Useful Pastimes,* followed in 1770, the title accurately reflecting its adherence to the Horatian *utile et dulce* formula, so critical to the Enlightenment. In general, the press expanded dramatically during this period, boasting about a hundred publications. The era simultaneously inaugurated the institution of the coffeehouse, then flourishing in England as a venue for the dissemination of culture and the appraisal of current developments. Likewise, the Cadet Corps, a military academy that trained young nobles in the spirit of the Enlightenment (where Tadeusz Kościuszko received his education), was founded in 1770. And the year 1773 marked both the dissolution by papal decree of the overly affluent Jesuit order, which had dominated schools and universities, and the creation of the Commission for National Education. The commission—the first ministry of education in Europe—elaborated a unified network of schools at all levels and appointed a Textbook Society to raise the quality of teaching materials. All of these innovations pursued a common goal: to rouse civic responsibility in

Poles, acquaint them with European trends, and instill in them values conducive to surmounting the country's sociopolitical disorder and cultural backwardness. Given the gentry's inertia, blind conservatism, and reluctance to sacrifice personal pleasures for communal needs, the expectations of authentic enlightenment seemed at best quixotic.

For the eighteenth century, the cornerstone of such enlightenment was, of course, a belief in the unity and immutability of reason, presumed to be essential and universal. The conviction (at the core of Deism, then in vogue) that reason, not divine revelation, is the effective agency in the acquisition of truth bred optimism about the feasibility of change. Hence the Enlightenment urged, through the exercise of reason, an interrogation of traditional doctrines; it emphasized individualism, freedom, and universal human progress; it favored the Newtonian method in science; and it posited functionalism as the criterion for truth. Astute advocates of the Enlightenment among Polish intellectuals, however, appreciated the need to adapt these principles to the specifics of Poland's situation. For example, the gentry's self-indulgent abuse of age-old liberties encouraged a questioning of tradition, yet suggested the wisdom of curbing individual license for the sake of national solidarity. Similarly, the concrete realities of Polish life modified the enthusiasm with which Poles could embrace the notion of universal human progress. Proponents of the Enlightenment in Poland propagated its tenets with an eye to practical, immediate application. In a sense, they responded to one of the Enlightenment's cardinal features: its analytical procedure, modeled on Newtonian scientific investigations, whereby one moves logically from observation of tangible phenomena to axioms and concepts. Among this active minority Krasicki played a prominent role.

Krasicki and the Enlightenment

A man of the Enlightenment par excellence, Krasicki was ideally endowed and positioned to execute his self-appointed task of transplanting enlightened ideas onto Polish soil. Adept at winning patronage from the powerful, Krasicki gravitated naturally toward seats of influence: he was Poniatowski's trusted chaplain and, as an involuntary Prussian subject in Warmia after the first Partition (1773), a favored associate of Frederick the Great. Both rulers esteemed his wit, intelligence, and administrative skills. As a result, Krasicki participated in the majority of significant cultural events that transpired in Poland during his lifetime. After completing theological studies in Vienna and Rome, he became a priest, a bishop, and finally an archbishop. At Poniatowski's invitation, he not only coedited and contributed to the *Monitor* for several years (1765–68, 1772) but also joined the Commission for National Education. For a while he served as president of his country's highest judicial court, the Crown Tribunal of Malopolska.

Krasicki's experiences in a wide range of fields intimately familiarized him with the professions and social classes whose shortcomings he satirized in essays published in the *Monitor* and in his *Fables and Parables* (1779, 1802), his Horatian *Satires* (1779, 1783), and other works composed during a burst of creativity in the 1770s. Like Jonathan Swift and Laurence Sterne, he perceived no conflict between a clerical career and literary activity. Indeed, the two occupations reinforced each other as related aspects of a larger subsuming imperative: to influence mores through the exhortations, ridicule, and exempla designed to expose error, deficiencies, and their pernicious consequences. Krasicki, who credited language with immense persuasive force, presupposed the social function of a writer, sharing Voltaire's notion that he should entertain his public while steering its thought ("teaching with a smile"). Satires paralleled sermons, then, in their pedagogical intent. The questions that interested the earthbound Krasicki were sooner ethical than metaphysical. His writings, in fact, have few traces of religiosity, despite his official religious affiliations. If the *Mouseiad* (1775), his first mock-heroic poem in the spirit of Alexander Pope's *Rape of the Lock* (1714), struck readers as unpriestly, then did, *a fortiori*, his *Monachomachia*, or *Monkiad* (1778). There, in a manner reminiscent of Boileau's *Le Lutrin* (1683), Krasicki the bishop lampoons Polish monastic orders as strongholds of superstition, despotism, and intemperate appetite (especially drunkenness). The ironic debunking measures how far Poland's religious representatives had departed from the Enlightened ideal—posited by negation in the mock epic—of a moral, learned, decorous citizen, a good Christian active in the affairs of his country.

Krasicki's oeuvre invites comparison with those West European models he blatantly emulated. His preferred genres reflect catholic Enlightenment tastes: journalism with a moralist slant (practiced by Swift, Voltaire); satire (à la Horace, Juvenal, Dryden, Pope, Swift, Voltaire); fable (of the La Fontaine variety); mock epic (in the style of Voltaire, Dryden, Pope); verse epistle (Horace, Pope); comedy (Molière, Denis Fonvizin); and history (Voltaire, Gibbon). By and large these writings are all of a piece, insofar as they evidence Krasicki's profound respect for education, reason, and moderation; his attachment to hierarchy as a reflection of a natural order; and his wit, balance, and common sense.

Krasicki's fondness for satire may be explained both by his temperament and by the times. Not unlike England during the heyday of English satire (1660–1745), eighteenth-century Poland was undergoing a radical shift in values, and partisans of oppositional groups found in the sardonic, sharp-edged expository style exemplified by the new science an ideal satiric medium for the thrust and parry of polemic. Clarity, conciseness, and symmetry were the literary virtues Krasicki most admired and strived for. Like Pope, Swift, and Voltaire, he ironized and derided excess and violence, but without the corrosive bite of his English and French counterparts. Tellingly, his satires contain no personal attacks and opt for genial urbanity over vitriolic diatribe. In that respect Krasicki resembles his idol Horace, whose down-to-earth practicality and affinity for the golden mean he also shared. While proselytizing for change, Krasicki, like his Roman predecessor, basically accepted the hierarchical structure of his society, wishing to redress its imperfections without undermining its foundations. To that end, Krasicki in his works pinpointed flaws and posited the general principles that would orient reformers in the proper direction for eradicating them.

"The Adventures of Mr. Nicholas Wisdom As Told by Himself"

During his lifetime Krasicki enjoyed vast popularity as the "Prince of Poets." From a modern perspective, however, his most mem-

orable contribution to Polish literature is arguably his authorship
of the first Polish novel, *The Adventures of Mr. Nicholas Wisdom*
(1776). This concise, fast-paced narrative, undertaken in part to
discredit the genre of romance then widespread in Poland, show-
cases Enlightenment values, particularly emphasizing the primacy
of education in the formation of character. Its didactic agenda is
neatly synthesized with a circumstantiated depiction of the Polish
petty gentry during the mid–eighteenth century and a treatment
of the major issues being debated by both Poland's and Western Europe's foremost intellectuals. Reprinted three times in as
many years, *The Adventures* met with an enthusiastic reception and
whetted the public's appetite for more novels, chiefly English and
French. Its translation into German (1776) and French (1818), in
turn, made the first Polish novel accessible to the rest of Europe
precisely when that genre, which earlier generations had dismissed
as lowly, was rapidly gaining esteem and a large audience.

The *Adventures* is read most fruitfully in the context of the
West European literature on which it drew heavily for inspiration
at a time when fiction was thoroughly cosmopolitan and the concept
of originality had yet to establish itself. As a novel of education
intent on teaching the "correct way to live," *The Adventures* has
much in common with Henry Fielding's *Tom Jones* (1749), Jean-
Jacques Rousseau's *Emile* (1762), and above all Voltaire's *Candide*
(1759). In fact, in conception, overall structure, tone, and specific
episodes, *The Adventures* unambiguously derives from Voltaire's
philosophical tale, although Krasicki deviates from his French predecessor in his use of retrospective first-person narration to bolster
the illusion of immediacy and verisimilitude. Both start with the
naive protagonist's early years on the ancestral estate that in microcosm typifies the flaws of the era. In Krasicki, these may be summed
up as the Sarmatism of the provincial gentry—their scant intellectual
resources; devotion to drinking, hunting, and gossip; and reliance
on emotions and superstitions as guideposts to behavior. Misfortune
stemming from their first romantic incident forces both Candide
and Nicholas to embark reluctantly on voyages that enable their
authors to expose the manifold follies not only of their respective
societies but also of humankind at large, while simultaneously
mocking their naïfs' callowness and untested idealism. In both, a

sustained hiatus in the hero's peregrinations takes the form of a fortuitous encounter with a utopian society whose attributes and potential limitations are assessed in light of his native country. After numerous further escapades, both Candide and Nicholas return home, all the wiser for their education in the "school of life." Having come full circle, they now contemplate their future from a more informed, empirically arrived-at position anchored in rational observation and common sense.

Apart from their shared belief in the tutelary nature of experience, more specific parallels between the two texts abound. By and large both confine characterization to the reductive sketchiness of types as manifestations of particular social or moral failings. Neither author individualizes his protagonist or the numerous secondary characters, who exist principally to instantiate ideas. To maintain readers' interest, both Voltaire and Krasicki move rapidly and in lapidary fashion, relying on the rhetorical devices of irony, understatement, hyperbole, parallelism, and contrast to make their points. Both authors provide their ignorant heroes with mentors and saviors: Candide's Leibnizian mentor Pangloss, his cynical foil Martin, and the sage of El Dorado are multiplied by Krasicki into a gallery of competing influences on Nicholas. The negative forces include his school tutor; his domestic French tutor, Damon; an unnamed habitué of salons; a court plenipotentiary (all in Poland), and the debauched Count Fickiewicz in Paris; while the positive are his maternal uncle, the Nipuan Xaoo, the old Inca, Quaker William, and the margrave de Vennes. All attempt to shape Nicholas's thinking by expounding their particular philosophies of life. Both heroes are duped out of money by one vulture after another, and in a concrete parallel, both fall victim to female cardsharps: Candide to the marquise de Parolignac and her daughter, Nicholas to the baroness de Grankendorff and her "daughters." For both authors, too, geographical expansion metaphorically signals potential pedagogical benefit—that is, mental and ethical growth. Finally, the conclusion of each work not only reunites the protagonist with the object of his first romantic transports (Candide with Cunégonde, Nicholas with Julie) but also distills the invaluable lesson acquired through experience: the necessity of engagement in one's appropriate arena of activity (Voltaire's famous "Il faut cultiver notre jardin"), which for both Voltaire and Krasicki means one's immediate environment. Usefulness and balance converge in disciplined occupation, for, as Voltaire's wise Turk avers, "Work keeps away from us three great evils: boredom, vice, and need." Although Voltaire's tale ends in low-key resignation while Krasicki's stresses its protagonist's more robust pleasure at having "found the way," the conclusions of both narratives imply a future governed by true and tried enlightened principles.

From the very opening of Book One, *The Adventures* launches its assault on several prevalent tendencies of the period that Krasicki also addressed in articles for the *Monitor:* miseducation, irrational treatment of children, aping of fashions, the habit of inconsequential gossip, and drunkenness—which Krasinski considered a decisive reason for Poland's downfall. Nicholas's parents typify the stultifying effects of the provincial gentry's complacent allegiance to unexamined traditions, perpetuated by inertia alone. Their deaths, which take place in Book One, are a prerequisite for Nicholas's maturation (and for the plot twists that motivate Nicholas's peripatetics). In the person of Damon, the private tutor hired for Nicholas's lessons, Krasicki satirizes both the pretentious, superficial foreign poseurs who then monopolized home education and the irresponsibility of the employers who foisted such incompetents on their offspring. Implicitly polemicizing with Rousseau, Krasicki here, as in various essays, opposes permissiveness in education, favoring instead a firm hand combined with a lucid mind and a stable temperament in the pedagogue, whose continuous supervision he deems much more critical than Rousseau proposed. Similarly, the deleterious effects of reading romances (defined in Book Two as "lying in a refined way") are ridiculed through the absurd yearnings and posturing, dramatized in the encounter with Julie, into which the impressionable Nicholas sinks after perusing the books recommended by Damon.

Once Nicholas reaches Warsaw, Krasicki turns his ironic pen to the extravagant waste, conspicuous consumption, spiritual poverty, and preference for veneer over essence that rule the urban way of life (captured in a sartorism probably deriving from Swift, and anticipating Thomas Carlyle). As Nicholas learns to the detriment of his purse, to be a "man about town" one must adopt the habits

of a licentious, indolent, foppish spendthrift. In the longest episode
of the first part, which transfers Nicholas to Lublin, Krasicki joins
the legion of satirists (e.g., Swift, Rabelais, Vasili Kapnist) who have
lashed out at antiquated and unjust legal systems tyrannized by
corrupt judges and inept, self-seeking lawyers. Bribes, personal
connections, and influential sponsors decide suits, travestying all
notions of justice. Before the favorable but illegally won ruling on
Nicholas's case is reversed, Krasicki unmasks his hero's profligacy
and blind prejudices through Nicholas's own sketchy journal of his
Parisian sojourn. Finally, having assailed an array of social types and
institutions on European soil, Krasicki, ever mindful of keeping his
readers' attention, shifts key. Nicholas's unexpected bankruptcy
owing to the loss of his estate prompts him to flee to Batavia in
the East Indies—a simple expedient allowing for a neat, economical
transition to the second, contrasting segment of the novel.

Aside from its debt to *Candide,* Krasicki's tripartite novel in its
individual sections exploits a number of specific texts and established
contemporary genres. Among the latter, the travelogue especially
enjoyed immense popularity in the eighteenth century, whose writers found it a convenient vehicle for social commentary. The chron-
otope of travel is particularly useful for propagandists of education,
since the geographical itinerary tropologically charts intellectual and
moral development through time-space. As in the science fiction
genre, direct acquaintance with other cultures and systems teaches
through the assimilation of differences and offers a yardstick by
which to gauge the merits and weaknesses of one's own society (in
Russian Formalist parlance, it enables "defamiliarization" [*ostra-
nenie*]). Nicholas's progress from the provinces (the village of
Szumin), through Warsaw, Lublin, then Paris, to the island of Nipu,
through Potosí, in present-day Bolivia, and Spain, with a return to
Paris and then to Szumin, gives him a sufficient sampling of national
and foreign cultures and of human types to alter, inevitably, his
sense of what is possible and desirable—what he can incorporate
into his own existence back home. Insofar as Nicholas himself is a
representative figure, his experiences allow Krasicki via his protagonist to place Polish mid–eighteenth-century thought and customs
in a wider context. That placement highlights simultaneously the
perils of parochialism and the wisdom of sustained interchange with

other civilizations, which, Krasicki cautions, should not degenerate into blind adoption of foreign habits or ignorance of one's own milieu.

Thus the convention of travel by definition provides both the comprehensive scope and the multiple perspectives on given issues and institutions that can expose defects from a fresh ("foreign" or "alien") viewpoint and can illustrate trenchantly the superiority of one way of life over others. By the 1770s scores of voyage tales with this multidimensionality had appeared, including *Candide*, Montesquieu's *Les Lettres persanes* (1721), Swift's *Gulliver's Travels* (1726), Henry Fielding's *Journal of a Voyage to Lisbon* (1755) and *Travels in the Two Sicilies* (1779–80), Samuel Johnson's *Rasselas* (1759), Tobias Smollett's *Travels in France and Italy* (1766), Sterne's *Sentimental Journey through France and Italy* (1768), and Aleksandr Radishchev's *Journey from St. Petersburg to Moscow* (1790). Like the majority of eighteenth-century English novels rooted in the picaresque tradition of *Lazarillo de Tormes* and Lesage, they all reaped the benefits of a broad social canvas against which to test the validity of concepts.

In its formative stages the literary genre of travel had close ties with both geographical and philosophical discoveries. Actual accounts of explorers in America, Africa, and the Orient stimulated not only further voyages but also fictional imitations that freely pilfered their anthropological details from real-life descriptions of distant, "exotic" civilizations. Their authors' preference for remote, little-known areas with a reputation for primitiveness contrasted with the sober, detailed notes by actual travelers (e.g., Addison, Shaftesbury, Gray, Gibbon, Casanova, Duclos, Dupaty) who had completed more mundane journeys, such as the Grand Tour institutionalized in England at this time (which Krasicki deplored as frivolous). Thus Madame de Graffigny's implausible, anachronistic *Lettres d'une Péruvienne* (1747), one of the era's best-sellers, relied on histories of the sixteenth-century Spanish conquest of Peru for information about the Incas. What realia her anachronistic epistolary novel contains probably derive from Garcilaso de la Vega's *Historia general del Perú* (1617), translated into French by 1704 and clearly a source for Book Two of Krasicki's novel, as well as a possible authority for Jean-François Marmontel's *Les Incas* (1778). Likewise,

Mademoiselle de la Roche-Guilhem's *L'Amitié singulière* (1710), set in Mexico, obviously gleaned facts about its polygamous customs at second hand. In general, the interplay between real travelogues, their interpolation into fiction to authenticate alien locales, and purely imaginative voyages in fantastic lands reached an unprecedented complexity that spilled over into the following century.

The imaginary voyages that proliferated throughout the early eighteenth century but eventually fell into oblivion had a markedly philosophical or satiric bent. The majority, including Pierre de Lesconvel's *Relation du voyage du prince de Montberaud dans l'Ile de Naudely* (1705), Mademoiselle Daunois's *Histoire véritable de Monsieur du Prat et de Mademoiselle Angélique* (1703), Guillaume Bougeant's *Voyage merveilleux du Prince Fan-Férédin dans la Romancie* (1735), and the abbé Prévost's *Histoire de la jeunesse du commandeur de* *** (1741), contain utopian elements. The narrative of a voyage by its very nature spawns the genre of island literature, with which utopian fiction frequently hybridizes. Both forms offer a respite from adventurous peregrinations, tending toward a more reflective, expository mode suitable for evaluating a given way of life. During the eighteenth century the authoritative text in island literature was undoubtedly Defoe's *Robinson Crusoe* (1719). Krasicki appropriated from it not only the island setting but also such specific moments as the protagonist's early sense of near-suicidal despair upon being washed ashore, his submergence in rewarding work, and, toward the book's end, the elaborate inventory of booty from Europe found on a shipwreck: in Krasicki's case, the haul included gold and silver items and several books, among them Molière's comedies, dozens of romances, a cookbook, and volume 3 of Newton's *Philosophy.* Finally, if Crusoe's island is, as Ian Watt has claimed, the utopia of the Protestant ethic, then the island of Nipu may be called the utopia of Enlightenment concepts.

Because the literary device of an island permits the portrait of a self-enclosed society isolated from corrupting neighboring forces, it has extraordinary potential as a utopia. Interest in the utopia beyond the horizon had revived with Renaissance explorations of the New World. A cult of primitivism in Europe followed the discovery of the Incan and Mayan civilizations in South and Central America, and myths about El Dorado and the Seven Cities of Gold, whose inhabitants reportedly basked in luxury and bliss, abounded in oral and written narratives. Political theorists, convinced that enlightened government represented the route to collective happiness, sought solutions in the ideal structures purportedly discovered by travelers. That trend culminated in Thomas More's *Utopia* (1516), which coined the neologism, derived from the Greek for the "perfect place" (*eu-topos*) or "no place" (*ou-topos*). Lacking the optimism of their humanist forebears, the enlightened skeptics of the eighteenth century stressed not human perfectibility, but imperfections, and so tended, like Swift, Johnson, and Bernard de Mandeville (*The Fable of the Bees,* 1714), to produce anti-utopias or dystopias. Krasicki, while sharing his contemporaries' respect for the authority of institutions rather than crediting humankind with limitless capacities for virtue, approached with a certain ambivalence the possibility of building a perfect society founded on reason and the golden mean.

Whether a synthetic utopian paradigm or individual texts served as Krasicki's point of departure for Book Two is difficult to determine. As scholars have attested, two works contained in his library undisputedly have direct pertinence to *The Adventures.* Several aspects of Tyssot de Patot's *Voyages et avantures de Jacques Massé* (1760), which subsequently became utopian *topoi,* surface in *The Adventures:* the newly arrived protagonist's inability to communicate in several European languages with the "natives" he encounters; his recourse to mimicry, which leads to mutual comprehension; his reliance on a beneficent older man, and so on. Krasicki's portrait of a primitive culture draws on *Histoires des Incas Rois du Perou,* the French translation of the Incan Garcilaso de la Vega's history. Since the Nipuans trace their roots to Peruvian ancestors, it makes sense that Krasicki would appropriate from Garcilaso such touches as the ceremony of ancestral baked bread, the islanders' adeptness at farming without metal tools, and the violent means of punishment for betrayal of one's country. In addition, Krasicki's treatment of the Nipuans shows evidence of possible borrowings from accounts of renowned utopias such as Book 4 of Plato's *Republic,*

More's *Utopia,* Francis Bacon's *Atlantis,* Thomas Campanella's *The City of the Sun,* the Brobdingnag sequence from Part 2 of *Gulliver's Travels,* and the El Dorado chapter in *Candide.*

Typically, little action transpires in utopias, for the genre's proposition of paradisal harmony and individual happiness precludes unrealized wants or a search for satisfaction of any kind. If, as René Girard and recent theorists have hypothesized, desire fuels the novel, then the dearth of unfulfilled longings robs the utopia of dynamism, substituting description and philosophizing for narrative momentum. Indeed, the supremely static second book of Krasicki's novel consists of a protracted exposition of the Nipuan minimalist philosophy by its spokesman Xaoo, and of Nicholas's reflections upon that way of life, programmatically contrasted with the norms of the "civilized" world. The form resembles a philosophical dialogue in a didactic, moralistic vein.

Krasicki's depiction of Nipuan society condenses many quintessential utopian features premised on the notion that people, like objects, may be subordinated to the laws of natural science. These include moderation in all spheres (no one among the Nipuans is crippled, obese, or overly thin); uniformity (all dress alike in robes that remain undifferentiated and unchanged, thereby eliminating preoccupation with appearance and the vagaries of fashion); egalitarianism (whereas More and Campanella portray collective societies, Krasicki follows Rousseau's *Social Contract* in the equal distribution of private property; all Nipuans own a house, a field, and a garden). Like More, Swift, and Voltaire, Krasicki makes the inhabitants of his utopia pacifists, and moreover, they are vegetarians. In fact, their inordinate fear of knives directly contradicts More's assertion in *Utopia* that one of mankind's necessities is metal, for the Nipuans reject metal as potentially dangerous and manage quite well with fish bone!

The cult of work common to utopias also exists on Nipu, and Nicholas, having no previous contact with physical labor, rapidly succumbs to its lure. In Nicholas's acquired appreciation for work, Krasicki presents the rudimentary beginnings of the disciplined, productive landowner that his protagonist will become upon his return to Poland. Nipuan society knows neither crime nor vice, nor the professions that evolved to adjudicate them (judges and lawyers, as in More). Similarly, just as in Swift, the ideal community lacks the word for evil, so the Nipuans have no vocabulary for specific wrongdoings such as lying, stealing, treachery, or flattery or (also as in Swift) for illnesses; the linguistic lacuna implies absence of the phenomenon. The sole violation adverted to (and recorded in the island's historical memory through the concrete case of Laongo) is betrayal, which carries the punishment of being stoned to death (a fate probably lifted from Garcilaso and possibly Campanella). Like Voltaire's El Doradians, the Nipuans have no need for money or valuables, or for tools that could serve as weapons, such as the knife from which they instinctively recoil.

Positing virtue as the goal of education, the islanders neither read nor possess any books, but they maintain a strong oral tradition, their poetry serving the religious function of praising God. For the Nipuans, as Xaoo explains, history consists not of accreted data, but of ethical training, whereby a legacy of moral precepts is bequeathed orally from one generation to the next. Neither philosophical speculation nor foreign lands and languages arouse the Nipuans' curiosity, for they recognize only practical knowledge. In their four-stage system of education, whose divisions parallel Rousseau's in *Emile*, the moderation, prudence, and reason that are instilled in a pupil by his sagacious teacher require not sophistication and book learning, but a personal experience of virtue.

The Nipuans anticipate Lev Tolstoy in their adherence to containment, excluding everything that could threaten the equilibrium of their existence through an artificial multiplication of needs. To ensure the inviolability of their simplified way of life, they shun external contacts and any novelty that portends change (the *Republic*, not accidently, argues that perfection enjoys "immunity to change"). In short, Nipuan society embraces the Platonic, or vertical, not the Aristotelian, or horizontal, principle of knowledge.

Like most utopias, Krasicki's defines itself in implicit contradistinction to imperfect existent societies, reprehends excess and uncontrolled emotions, favors stasis (what Evgenii Zamiatin's dystopic *We* calls entropy), and completely bypasses the dark, irrational aspects of human nature. It presupposes the desirability of certainty, timelessness (the genre is profoundly antihistorical), and a uniform epistemology. Self-contained though the Nipuan episode is, both geographically and philosophically, Krasicki pointedly orchestrates resonances between it and Book One through antitheses and parallels. For instance, the Nipuan system of education expounded by Xaoo dramatically contrasts with Nicholas's schooling; the dignified, honest settlement of a boundary dispute between two Nipuans casts into greater relief the cynical corruption accompanying Nicholas's legal suit; the tranquil joy amid which the Nipuans feast on bread as they celebrate God and their forefathers renders the drunken rowdiness of gatherings in Book One all the more repellent, and so forth. Yet as several commentators have observed, by the time Nicholas abandons the island, impressed but not fully persuaded by Xaoo's preachings, the reader's relief surpasses the protagonist's, for the reductive perfection of Krasicki's utopia makes for a sluggish narrative. It leads one to appreciate all the more Voltaire's discretion in condensing Candide's visit to El Dorado into only a few pages.

After the comparative immobility of Book Two, the final section of Krasicki's novel almost overwhelms the reader by the breathless speed at which its dramatic succession of misadventures unfolds. Geographically, characterologically, and thematically Krasicki encompasses an immense range: Rescued at sea by the tyrannical captain of a Spanish slave ship, Nicholas travels in fetters to the gold mines in Potosí. He is eventually extricated by the American philanthropist Quaker William and sails to Buenos Aires. Leaving on a ship commanded by the margrave de Vennes, he disembarks at Cádiz, where he is imprisoned by members of the Spanish Inquisition, who move him to an insane asylum in Seville. Saved and aided by de Vennes—a secular version of divine intervention—he returns to Poland through Madrid and Paris. As Nicholas hurtles through these melodramatic ordeals, they lead him to ruminate on Xaoo's credo, thereby affording Krasicki ample opportunity to subject the utopian teachings of Book Two first to apparent confirmation, then to revision and refinement. If initially the Spanish captain's monetary greed, the disinterested charity of Quaker William, and the cruel indifference of the Spanish Church officials all seem to corroborate Xaoo's clear-cut notions of morality, a corrective eventually is supplied by the margrave de Vennes, who supplements Xaoo's sagacity with practical counsel.

The cosmopolitanism of the polished young sea captain provides a stylistic contrast with Xaoo that his ideas corroborate on the philosophical plane. De Vennes exposes the impracticality of utopia, supplanting the abstractness of its schematic universalism (which Krasicki criticized directly in articles for the *Monitor*) with a flexible set of tenets that take into account individual cultural differences. The margrave's disquisition on well-intentioned idealists underscores the stifling repressiveness of utopists: by legislating conduct according to *a priori* blueprints, they proceed from knowledge not of how people are, but of how they wish them to be. Since "children of nature" can be children only *in* nature, Xaoo's philosophy has limited application for the "civilized" world, as Nicholas discovers when he expounds Nipuan ideas in Spain and Poland. Unlike the xenophobic Nipuans, who must retreat into defensive isolation to uphold their uncompromising beliefs, de Vennes can maintain his moral code wherever his international wanderings take him, precisely because his expectations are firmly anchored in the specifics of highly divergent experience rather than in dreams of universal perfection. Convinced that "a generalization [about a nation] is nothing more than prejudice against shared character traits of nations," de Vennes urges and practices the thoughtful discrimination that enables him not only to reconcile the general with the individual but also to accommodate the human irrationality and inconsistency that defied the Nipuan imagination (e.g., the Dostoyevskian insight that "it can be harder to cope with happiness than unhappiness"). Although the house Nicholas builds on his recovered estate in honor of Xaoo commemorates the "sacred precepts" of his Nipuan teacher, Nicholas ultimately attains a "happy and virtuous" life by heeding de Vennes's sensible advice: he accepts dissenting viewpoints, confines his intimate circle to a few select friends, tries to fulfill his responsibilities as a citizen, and turns his administrative talent to running an efficient, humane estate. Xaoo's radical notions prove adaptable to Polish Enlightenment society only when modified by the margrave's tolerance and experiential orientation.

Like Voltaire's Candide and (on a smaller geographical scale) Fielding's Tom Jones, Krasicki's Nicholas must roam the world to learn, paradoxically, that "home is best." Just as paradoxically, it is his journey that furnishes the insights and skills required to make the most of "home." In that critical regard Nicholas represents progress over his parents, whose dedication to the status quo was simply an automatic obscurantist reflex. Nicholas's contentment springs partially from his newfound ability to tread the golden mean, to find a fruitful middle ground between categories that formerly appeared mutually exclusive: individual and community, tradition and innovation, work and pleasure, sentiment and thought, magnanimity and profit. Having learned to relish private joys, yet, in de Vennes's words, "to live among men," Nicholas becomes Krasicki's model for the Polish gentry. Indeed, the pattern of Nicholas's integration into his "natural" environment coincides with the image of a good life that emerges in Krasicki's correspondence: a calm domestic regimen, shaped by the civilizing forces of moderation and good sense, in which one pursues the simple tasks of everyday life, cultivates temperate pleasures, and discharges those obligations for which one is equipped. That ideal finds more detailed embodiment in Krasicki's lengthier quasi novel, *The Squire* (1778–1803).

Like his West European contemporaries, Krasicki in his essays advocated a pristine, direct style, which his own works exemplify. His predilection for clarity and conciseness accounts for the simplicity of his classical prose, inflected by irony but unencumbered by the florid embellishments of the late Baroque, which violated his sense of taste. Similarly, his affinity for balance manifests itself in the novel's symmetrical structure. More or less equal in length, the three books comprise self-contained units, linked, however, by recurrent themes, motifs, and types. Books One and Three, with their energetic narrative and eloquent portrayal of contemporary Polish reality, flank the static ideal projected in the middle section. Motifs that in the first book carry negative associations or consequences reappear in Book Three, but in a favorable light: the romance with Julie that occasions separation and "exile" culminates ten years later in an auspicious marriage; Nicholas's irresponsible self-gratification as an adolescent on the family estate is countered in maturity by his benevolence and effectiveness in managing the property; whereas his early lawsuit unearths ugly corruption among those entrusted with upholding justice, his later case is decided favorably because unobstructed impartiality triumphs. Implicit in the very movement of Krasicki's novel, as in *Tom Jones,* is a sanguine but qualified trust in the possible victory of goodness on an individual basis and in human receptivity to rational argument when buttressed by the immediacy of experience.

In its brevity and good-natured equanimity *The Adventures* consciously eschews extremes. It lacks the bite of *Candide,* the venomous sting of *Gulliver's Travels,* the sprawling breadth and rollicking zest of *Tom Jones*—three of the many sources to which it is indebted. Its restraint and derivative aspect should not obscure the considerable historical and aesthetic merits of *The Adventures.* The novel provides a vivid sense of the dilemmas plaguing mid–eighteenth-century Poland, situating them in the broader context of the Enlightenment debate about knowledge, education, religion, and morality waged by the foremost minds of the era. Its narrative drive, unadorned yet expressive language, and deft irony make it an eminently readable text even for those indifferent to the questions it raises. Moreover, as the first Polish novel, *The Adventures* suggested directions and offered a model of sorts for subsequent forays in the genre, including Adam Mickiewicz's superb novel in verse, *Pan Tadeusz* (1834), and Bolesław Prus's memorable *The Doll* (1887). Finally, the authentically cosmopolitan nature of *The Adventures* encourages its incorporation into the established fund of European eighteenth-century fiction from which so far it has been excluded—presumably because the original language makes it inaccessible even to most educated readers. Hence the appearance of this first English translation of the novel that debuted in Poland more than two centuries ago is not only welcome but also long overdue.

Helena Goscilo

THE ADVENTURES OF
MR. NICHOLAS WISDOM

Foreword

A foreword is to a book what an entrance hall is to a house, with, however, one difference: it is hard for a house to be without an entrance hall, while a book can manage without a foreword. Forewords were unknown to classical authors. Their invention, like that of many other superfluous things, is the work of later centuries.

The reasons authors place forewords at the beginning of their works are manifold. Some, suffused with false modesty, confide to the reader (who of course has not asked) that certain friends of great importance and no less esteem forced them to publish what had been written solely for self-satisfaction, what they wished to keep out of public view. Others complain of betrayal; the manuscript was carried off against their will. A third group, gratifying the bidding of their elders, have made a heroic offering of obedience in publishing the book. These forewords and others like them make confidential disclosures to the yawning reader as if they were of great interest to him.

Forewords came imperceptibly into fashion. Now, however, that fashion reigns supreme because the art of writing has become a trade. For a great number—I am told the better part—of my fellow writers make a living from publishing. So now we make books like watches. Since their quality depends largely on their thickness, we try to expand, lengthen, and inflate our works as much as possible. The shrewd reader thus can easily surmise how much forewords benefit the literary trade.

In addition to the reasons stated above, there are various other motives that prompt, and sometimes impel, the writing of forewords.

Frequently an author confides his objective to the reader, his intent in writing the book. Surely confidentiality so exemplary and so felicitous is worthy of both respect and gratitude. How else would the reader be able to surmise that a prayer book was written for devotional purposes, a comedy to make one laugh, a tragedy to make one cry, or a history for learning about events of yore? Certainly he would be uncertain, would have doubts. Had not the benevolent author magnanimously warned him, he might have laughed at a tragedy, wept while reading a comedy; he might have taken a prayer book for romance and prayed from a chronicle.

There are authors aware how refined their own work is and how shallow the intelligence of other people may be. Filled with compassion for the herd of ordinary readers, they deign to degrade themselves, to stoop for the common good, explaining in the foreword what is difficult to comprehend in that which follows. I, for my part, while greatly admiring their intellectual grandeur, am so audacious, however, as to advise them to write *postscripta* instead of forewords. One usually reads a foreword before reading the book. The reader thus finds at the very outset difficulties simplified that he yet knows nothing about, complexities explained he has not yet heard of. And the result? Terrified and not knowing where to turn, the reader abandons the book and, with untold harm to humankind, remains his original savage self.

When an author encourages the reader with promises, the foreword becomes a subtle encomium of the work. Then, in order to avoid being a braggart, the author ingeniously alters his character. Now he is a chum who outrages a friend with his modesty, now a printer who has written the foreword without the author's knowledge, now a man of letters, unknown to both, who, having learned of the anticipated appearance of so useful a work in print and having by chance read the manuscript, cannot help but express his satisfaction.

There are melancholy voices who wail in elegiac fashion about the ignorance, the blindness, the ingratitude of this "iron" age. In such a mournful foreword the author does not praise himself but, full of fitting modesty, lets it be known that he has fallen upon hard times, that had he lived in Athens or Rome, statues might have been erected to him...that it is lamentable he was not born earlier. *Tantae-ne animis coelestibus irae.*[1]

There are—I note sorrowfully—those authors who follow the example of the Spanish knight and make giants out of windmills. They are angry in the manner of the Prophets. Before anyone has read their work they chide the Zoiluses.[2] Not content to mount a single attack, they abuse all those who are biased, inattentive, frivolous, superficial, envious, and stupid. Naturally, the biased, inattentive, superficial, frivolous, envious, and stupid are all those who will not accept and adore them.

There is yet another kind of author who stands in marked contrast with those described above. This is the author who is convinced of his own imperfection or who simply pretends to be convinced of it, so as to arouse not admiration as much as compassion. Trembling and on bended knee (as Boileau says), in a humble foreword such authors desire to make amends and apologize to the displeased and even more bored reader.[3] They strive in vain. In this corrupt and utterly polluted age of ours the worst misdeed can be forgiven, but to be boring is an unpardonable sin. I would advise such authors not to write at all. But writing is an incurable disease.

Unworthy associate of this honorable craft, I myself developed several projects for other books before finishing this one. If it meets with approval, I will gratefully accept the reader's kind judgment. If not, I will be chagrined, but I will continue to write.

BOOK ONE

Chapter One

Let it be known in advance to anyone who reads this description of my life that what follows is neither confession nor panegyric. I have undertaken this task neither for empty glory nor for self-mortification. Instead, having free time while staying in the country, I choose to write rather than rush headlong after a hare or seek gout in a tankard.

I was born into a family of respectable gentry. In what year I will not say, for that is of no use to anyone. Chronology is not at all necessary to my story, and besides, it is not very pleasant to remind myself that I am old. Had I wished to trace my ancestry using those testimonials in the graduation addresses[4] and panegyrics attributed to my forebears (which to this day hang rotting on the walls of my home chapel), I would perhaps have found myself related by blood to all the ruling families of Europe. However, I am quite removed from that type of vanity. Niesiecki included us in his book of genealogies to spite Paprocki and Okolski,[5] and I happened to read in one old manuscript that during the famous Gliniane Rebellion of 1379, one Gabriel Wisdom carried the horsehair-tasseled ensign before Raphael Granowski, marshal and royal high hetman of the time.

Before I speak about my upbringing, a few words ought to be said about those to whom I owe my origin, namely, my father and my mother. My father—first a purse-bearer, then constable, later sword-bearer, lord of the hunt, cup-bearer, and finally pantler—saw his sixty years of service to district and province, his constant travels to electoral and administrative assemblies, happily rewarded at the end of his days with the crowning achievement of being made lord high steward. The degree of respect he had earned was so great that he was nearly made an associate judge, but fate, heedless of virtue, prevented him from assuming that rank. It was not long before he reconciled himself to this, however, by reflecting, as is customary to those who suffer misfortune, on the vagaries of this world. An extremely pleasant disposition helped him to achieve this reconciliation: he was the type of person commonly called a kind soul.

Father knew nothing of the deeds of the Greeks and Romans, and if he had heard anything about Czech and Lech,[6] then it was probably from a church homily. What his father (who, it was maintained, possessed an even more admirable soul than he) told him, he also told us over and over, namely, that our manner of speaking and thinking was inherited along with the land. In sum, Father was a straightforward, sincere, friendly person. And although he could not define virtue, he did know how to practice it. Because of his inability to define virtue, however, he had a somewhat mistaken notion of kindness: he thought that being hospitable to a guest in your house meant to get drunk with him. As a result of this, his wealth was diminished and his health impaired. He nonetheless bore his gout heroically, and during the times it did not bother him, he would often repeat that it was his pleasure to suffer for his beloved fatherland.

My mother, brought up entirely in the country, I daresay had visited the towns nearby only on church festivals. Anyone can easily deduce from this that she lacked many of the accomplishments of today. Not that this concerned her in the least. Once when she was chided by a gallant for appearing to have overly strict principles and a certain primitiveness offensive to those in high society, she told him with heartfelt sincerity that common virtue was preferable to polite vice.

The earliest years of my childhood were spent in the company of women. Nurses and nannies interpreted my as yet poorly articulated words to be extraordinarily sagacious responses. They were reported immediately, and with great eagerness, to my mother, who, in turn, would launch into a discourse about them on any given social occasion. Neighbors would nod in agreement, yawning, and not a few would finally have begun to doze, had Father not kept them awake with frequent rounds of drinks. Thus braced, the neighbors would pay abundant compliments, make entreaties and predictions, while my father would weep.

Over the ensuing years I have concluded more than once that my earliest education was perverse. And I have also pondered how evil and harmful it is to entrust even small children to unenlightened individuals. I heard far too many fables and dreadful romances. To this day my head is full of them. Although a thoroughly rational man, I frequently must struggle with myself not to lend credence to sorcery and superstition or to rid myself of some fear or other and not abhor the dark or solitude. Furthermore, a penchant for slander developed imperceptibly in me. Hearing the women censure the manners of everyone in the household and knowing that their tales were warmly received by the adults of the family, I made it a point to win the good graces of Mother or the head maid by regaling them with all sorts of things about the others. If there was nothing on which to base such talk, I made it up. I noted too how conversations in the evening tended to be about ghosts, witches, and evil spirits and those in the morning about dreams. One of the women would tell another what she had dreamed, and from their interpretations and divinations I learned that when someone dreams of fire, one should expect guests in the house, and if in the dream one loses a tooth, a relative undoubtedly will die.

Thus my life continued until, when I was seven years of age, my mother's brother happened to pay us a visit. He was a man notable for the office he held, for his education, and for his knowledge of the world. I observed my uncle closely, especially because I saw that my parents showed him great respect. I marveled that, having stayed with us for two days, not once did he become intoxicated. He did not deign to believe what our cleric said about ghosts. He became repugnant to me because he was not amused by my behavior the way others were. To make matters worse, he did not respond at all to Mother's exaggerated praise of me but, on the contrary, perplexed me greatly by asking whether I knew how to read and write, and whether I possessed other skills appropriate to one my age. This was the first time I had ever heard words to this effect. At first Mother tried to shift the conversation to another topic, but finding that this made him pursue his inquiry further, she stated—and I can still remember what she said almost word for word—"I know you will be surprised, dear brother, when I tell you quite candidly that our little Nickie does not yet know how to read or write. But you will not reproach us for this when I tell you the reasons we have not wanted to rush his education. First of all, the child is sensitive, weak; excessive sitting, which is so very necessary for learning the ABC's, might have harmed him. Then too, as you yourself can see, he is extremely fearful. If we had found him a tutor, his spontaneity would have been sacrificed, and once spontaneity is lost, it cannot be recovered. It would be difficult to find an individual as ideal as we would have liked for Nickie's education. And finally, you know the saying, 'It does no good to break in a young colt.'"

"Well said, my dear," Father responded. "My late father (may he rest in peace) said the very same thing about me. But just the same, if your brother says so, it would probably be best to put Nickie in school. Be so kind as to name the place and person. For the present, let us drink to the health of this gentleman, honored sir, and beloved benefactor."

It would be difficult to express the joy I—and perhaps also my mother—felt when our common enemy left the following day. His words, however, made a fatal impression on my father. Over and over he would begin discoursing on schools. A primer and a slate were even purchased. This pained Mother immeasurably. However, since she was a God-fearing woman and had been reproved for pampering me to death, she made what certainly must have been the most heroic sacrifice of her life by permitting me to be sent to grammar school. To grammar school because Father stubbornly and with great tenacity criticized domestic education, maintaining that there was no such tradition in Poland.[7] I do not remember what Mother's response was to this. What I know and will always remember is that in the end, after protracted squabbles, qualms, farewells, and blessings, I was sent off to school, shedding bitter tears.

Chapter Two

Before describing the further course my schooling took, permit me to reflect on certain matters, especially my state of mind at the time. After seven years, not so much of upbringing as of pampering, I was devoid not only of learning but also of any notion whatsoever that my wishes could be opposed. Hence this first instance of involuntary departure seemed unbearable to me. I was being introduced for the very first time to the yoke of subordination. For the first time I was being removed from the company of my parents, from the caresses of my mother, from the servants' adulation.

What, however, horrified me most (as I remember) was the reason for which I was being dispatched: education. I could hardly consider it something good, since I was threatened with it as though it were a punishment. I thus came to the conclusion that it could not help but be something unpleasant and painful. Having never seen anyone in our house read from a book except in church, I had supposed that the happiness of adults was founded on not having to study. My apprehension was heightened by the lament-filled farewells of members of the household who felt sorry because the young master was being sent off to study. Although my parents said that learning would be beneficial for me, I decided they were merely trying to alleviate my misery, being convinced in my heart of hearts that education was a punishment I deserved and that this was why I was being sent away to school.

The long-desired tutor turned out to be a totally inexperienced young man, himself still a student. He was the nephew of the father superior at the school to which I was going. My servant, someone I had long known, was the son of our steward. He was about the same age as I and a faithful and inseparable companion in every escapade at home. Completing the entourage were an old store-keeper and a housekeeper trained in the secrets of home remedies—this for the restoration of my health should I fall ill, God forbid.

On the eve of my departure I was summoned to Father, together with the tutor, and was made to witness the instructions given the latter. I understood then how kind souls are capable of readily accepting ideas completely opposite to their inclinations. For having first bestowed parental authority on the tutor, my father begged him by all that he held dear not to be lenient with me. Loudly singing the praises of the lash, he mustered up, as if for the first time, a quotation that came directly from a primer: "Spare the rod and spoil the child." Time and again he used glorious adages like this to punctuate the rather brief sections of his orations. Finally, presumably as a sign of his right to punish me, he placed in the tutor's hand a little whip, small and thin to be sure, but as I was later to learn from experience, most painful. As we were leaving the room, he half opened the door and, as if having forgotten the thing that was most vital, called out to the tutor: "Flog him well, 'cause that's what I'm paying you for!"

One can well understand how I felt then, how terrified I was, how I trembled and wept. I immediately ran to Mother and told her everything that had happened, sobbing bitterly all the while. She summoned the tutor and in very few words made him understand that if her child were touched, he would be dismissed and answer with his hide as well. This provided me some consolation.

We set out the very next day. I moaned nearly the whole trip, while my tutor presumably pondered whether he should obey the master or the mistress.

We reached our destination without mishap and were received with considerable joy. The beginnings of my school life were uneventful. Though I possessed great intelligence, I possessed an even greater aversion to study. My tutor, recalling the threats of the mistress more than the commands of the master, at first was gentle with me. But having received a lashing from his own professor, he got so heated that, although I was innocent, he gave the same to me—only twice as hard. From then on he satisfied alternately the obligations *both* my parents had imposed: lavishing praise without reason, beating without cause. Upon receiving a set of clothing as a gift from Mother on his name day, he wrote my parents posthaste that Master Nicholas would have surpassed even Hercules in learning.

My subsequent experiences in school differed very little from the initial one. The comradeship of my schoolmates, and even more

our joint participation in sundry gambols, often produced less notable though no less injurious results.

I had reached my sixteenth year when I received news of my
father's death and orders to return home immediately. To be sure,
I experienced a natural feeling of sorrow, but once this was assuaged,
the alluring prospect of freedom presented itself to me. Welcomed
home as a long-awaited guest, I now began to enjoy the adoration
of the household in double measure. The tutor even attested that
I no longer needed to attend school. The neighbors added their
support to so sound an opinion, persuading Mother that I had
attained precisely the right age to make myself worthy of my peers'
affection and to lend support to the popular Wisdom family fame
to which I was heir.

With this in mind, I put in a generous supply of ammunition
in the form of beer, mead, wine, and hard liquor and began to
welcome people to my home. Mother did not view this way of life
favorably at first, especially after my ribs were injured slightly when
a sled turned over on me during a sleighing party. Bribed with
promises and gifts, however, the members of the household were
able to cover up some of my escapades. Those they could not gloss
over were given at least a neutral appearance. The heady days of
that sweet life would have continued had not my uncle, appointed
guardian in my father's will, rent the fabric of my happiness.

The uncle arrived and displayed no revulsion, and I was beginning to feel triumphant. Then suddenly, pale and trembling from
fear, my valet, a former servant I had only recently promoted, came
running up to me and announced that every one of my hounds,
pointers, and greyhounds, used along with the mongrels to bring
big game to bay, had been drowned in the pond and that some of
the horses had been taken to another village and others sent to
auction. The huntsmen had been dismissed. And worst of all, the
Cossack bandore player had been ignominiously expelled from the
house and given a painful viaticum for the road.

I was summoned to my uncle's room and confronted there by
both him and Mother. Overwhelmed by shame, anger, bitterness,
and humiliation, I had to listen to reprimands, like it or not. Once
again rules were laid down for me to follow. I was forced to make

a virtue out of necessity: I pledged to change my way of life, inwardly resolving not to fulfill one iota of what I had promised.

Either the neighbors found out about this row or certain gentlemen were purposely apprised of it, for I did not see one of my former comrades during the whole of my uncle's rather protracted sojourn with us. Instead, only sensible, educated, and sober people whom I had not known before made merry with me. And I noticed that the amusements I pursued with them, though not so jolly and uproarious as the things I had done before, nonetheless had greater continuity and unobtrusively gave rise to new amusements. After the old teacher was banished, a new one could not be found on short notice. Uncle meanwhile had set out on a long journey. A female neighbor who had recently arrived from Warsaw was thus able to convince my mother that what was needed for a young man my age was not a Latin tutor—they were for schoolboys—but a tutor who could teach French and, even more important, impart good manners and breeding. She then proceeded to recommend for this post a young Frenchman who was staying with her. This young man, although he had entered her service as a valet, had done so purposely (according to him) in order to disguise his famous name. Otherwise he would have been recognized and made to answer for slaying the *premier président* of Parliament in a duel that had taken place at Versailles under the very eyes of the king.

Chapter Three

During the first days of the tutor's stay with us, that is, before he became well acquainted with everyone in the household, there was a general display of politeness, with particular respect being shown to Mother. For our part, we tried as hard as we could not to appear bumpkins and simpletons in the eyes of M. le Marquis. And M. Damon (who revealed that he was a marquis but requested that we not honor him with this title, lest he be detected) graced us with more and more forms of special politeness, the likes of which had never been seen in our parts.

After a few days, Mother implored him to recount his experiences. At first most reluctant to do so, he eventually was prevailed upon—but not without receiving beforehand a number of gifts. He disclosed to us his near-royal birth, incredible adventures at sea and on land, amorous encounters—some favorable, others with bad consequences, the most ill-starred leading ultimately to the duel with Parliament's *premier président*. He finished his tale, beseeching us by all that we held dear not to betray him. Since he had revealed himself to us, his life was in our hands. He had already learned from a close friend and prince that the king of France had written to our king with the request that he be sought out in Poland. We promised M. le Marquis absolute protection in our house, warning him, however, that he would be regarded as a tutor, except in private social gatherings, where he would be received as a family friend and a gentleman worthy in every respect.

Mother could hardly conceal her great satisfaction at having found, with so little effort, such a treasure for her house. But as M. le Marquis's secret weighed somewhat on her conscience, she, being cautious and extremely discreet, confided it to only two neighbors of tested prudence and then only after making them swear solemnly not to divulge it. And when rumor spread throughout the region about M. le Marquis's awe-inspiring adventures, she could not comprehend how this had happened. Everyone, however, had been properly discreet: they had gabbed about his adventures only at private social gatherings. Several skeptics emerged, but there were also ladies who knew how to curb this vestige of Sarmatian uncouthness. These were ladies who were inclined by nature to be compassionate and who looked with much regret on the degradation of so illustrious a person as M. le Marquis.

I found the new tutor greatly to my liking, first and foremost because he presented my mother with clear and unmistakable proof that learning was fit only for schoolboys. The intelligence of so illustrious a little master as I, on the other hand, if hampered by rules, would serve little purpose except to make me the object of ridicule in Paris.

"Among us in Paris," he imparted, "the Latin language is held in such contempt that people who know it are not allowed to appear in polite society. Ladies look askance at such people, and gallants term them pedants. A good education begins with the acquisition of bearing and dash, it develops and progresses with the study of a lordly, refined manner of thinking, and finally it comes to fruition with experience in feelings of the heart."

I must confess I did not understand in the least this educational scheme, and perhaps Mother did not either. Nevertheless, it seemed to us to be so fine, clever, and useful that everyone was most content with my being trained in lordliness of thought and in the experience of feelings of the heart. Mastery of the French language could not be neglected in this process, however, because without it (as M. Damon maintained) one could not expect to possess feelings or be lordly.

My uncle had left behind a French grammar. The next morning I presented it to M. Damon so that he could begin giving me lessons. I was extremely surprised by his response: "I think," he announced, "that you need only study feelings in a thorough manner. I mentioned not long ago that rules hamper the intellect. What is grammar if not a collection of rules? Abandon this schoolboy's tool and follow the path of high society. A gallant's learning is reflected in his ability to make small talk with his peers. Henceforth your lessons will consist solely in small talk with me. From it you will acquire a knowledge of things, and the feelings of a gallant are what you will practice."

I was so delighted by Damon's response that I thought I had already mastered everything. We began at once to bring the projected plan to fruition. It should be noted here that in a fairly short time I had begun to grasp, then to comprehend, and finally also to speak French rather well.

Chapter Four

Since I had become skilled not only in understanding but also in speaking French, M. Damon thought it vital that we avail ourselves of volumes of love and morals so that I might gain even greater fluency in that language and acquire the rudiments of feelings. In the house, besides *The Heroine, A Turtledove's Voice,* and *The Little Altar of Fragrant Incense,* there was not a single book to be found.[8]

After great effort on M. Damon's part and several months' waiting, romances about Cyrus and Clélie at last arrived. These vast, protracted stories did not frighten me in the least. Indeed, I acquired such a taste for hearing M. Damon read them that, wondering how a complicated intrigue would finally end, I was sometimes prey to sleepless nights, the magnificent Alcander or the faithful Mandane ever on my mind. Filled with feelings of heroism and not having yet experienced a Dorine, or a Cléomire, oh, did I sigh and find fault with the gods.[9] To make my doleful moans more resonant, I stole many a time to a copse not far from our manor.

Once, while lying on a soft grassy slope reading the most doleful chapter of the story of Hippolyte,[10] I began to cry out in a doleful voice: "Why won't you take pity on me, dear Julie? How can you be so cruel to one who would admit to being the happiest man alive if he could but become your eternal servant... Say the word! I am prepared to do anything you wish. Would that you did not choose to persecute me so mercilessly! For you I would be willing to go anywhere on earth!"

"Oh dear Sir! Do not do me this injustice," said a young ward of my mother who was standing near me at that moment. She had the very same name, Julie, and, while walking through the copse, had chanced upon me just as I summoned up these heroic exclamations.

"I do not understand," she went on, "why my behavior should annoy anyone, let alone the son of the woman who has become a mother to me, an orphan!"

I do not know whether it was this curious incident, Julie's charming voice, the blush that accompanied it, or an imagination made distraught by romances, but at that moment she seemed to me a goddess. I fell at her feet; my tears bathed her hands. I pledged her eternal love. And had she not forcibly torn herself from me, I know that whatever Cyrus told Mandane and Hippolyte, Julie, she

would have heard from me in its entirety as I made my debut into
the world of sensual experience. My great respect for her, however,
did not allow me to disobey her command.

I remained in that same spot, and once she had passed from
my sight, I began conversing with brook, trees, and knolls. Imitating
any and all originals that happened to occur to me, I did not omit
even the smallest circumstances surrounding first encounters that
I had learned from reading romances.

Until this time Julie's beauty, though exquisite, had not made
a great impression on me. Accustomed to seeing her, I kept well
within the bounds of respect proper to the fair sex. This curious
incident seemed to be an extraordinary instance of predestination;
Julie's every emotion affected my heart. And since my heart now
really had a true object, it was no longer attracted to fictional
adventures. When I came home, I noticed that Julie's face had
become flushed and that when I entered, she lowered her eyes.
Not being yet fully aware of the signs of genuine romance, I
assumed that my indiscretion had aroused ire. The thought of this
saddened me so much that I was unusually gloomy and distracted
and looked forward with anticipation to the night so that I might
rest peacefully and thus lighten the affliction of my heart. The night
was passed virtually in sleeplessness. Julie—now as I had seen her
in the copse, now angry—was constantly before my eyes. And when
at last overcome by sleep, my eyelids closed, I dreamed again and
again of her charming and pleasant figure.

Chapter Five

If I wanted to describe the beauty of the one I had grown fond
of, following in the footsteps of other lovers, I would tire readers
with a depiction much too long and drawn out. Lilies and roses,
pearls and rubies, Diana's figure, Venus's grace, doubtless would
be de rigueur. Real beauty, however, needs no embellishment.
Moreover, my plain, forthright style would not be equal to the

task. Julie did not possess that radiance that, as they say in romances, makes lilies envious. Still, I do not wish to be unjust to the rose or the lily, and so I shall simply say that she was fair, had a rosy complexion, that what was most pleasing of all about her personality was her unusual modesty. Her dark eyes were vivacious and full. But they did not wander to the left or to the right, nor were they flirtatious. Her gait was measured, though not heavy; her voice graceful without being artificial. Perhaps these would be considered shortcomings by others, but she had won my heart.

Not far from our manor was a wide pond. Mother and Julie had gone on a stroll in that direction and were walking in the shade of trees planted on the dam. I meanwhile noticed a small boat near one bank. I got in it and pushed off. As I was nearing the very middle, Mother called to me. I tried to change the boat's course too abruptly. It listed so suddenly that I lost my balance and, falling into the water, went under. The servants immediately came running. They hauled me out onto the shore nearly half drowned. They did this with great trouble and at great risk, and not before I had gone under more than once.

When I first opened my eyes after coming to, I saw that Julie was weeping. This produced in me such strong emotion that I fainted a second time. Only after being taken home and put to bed did I regain consciousness. Once I had recovered, I diligently sought ways to see Julie. When I asked Mother about her, she said that my second indisposition had frightened Julie so much that she had swooned, and it had proved well-nigh impossible to revive her. Now she was gaining strength, resting in her own room. If Julie's infirmity gave me reason for sorrow, the cause of the infirmity put vigor into my veins. The consequences, whether of fright or of the cold, were so great, however, that I could not get out of bed for several weeks. Throughout my infirmity Mother was almost always at my side.

Once when Mother left the room, she directed Julie to stay with me, saying that she would return very shortly. When I saw Julie alone, in the absence of witnesses, the fear and confusion I felt were so great that I hardly dared open my lips. However, overcoming my shyness, I said in a shaking voice: "Can I indeed hope that my impulsiveness, perhaps improper, will be forgiven?...

Will your faith in me grow if I swear a hundred times to fulfill that which I promised?"

At first my question was met with silence. My eyes fixed on her, I waited for a pronouncement that would seal my fate. Finally, with a deep sigh, she managed to utter the following reply: "It does not seem to me that it would be good for the house in which I live largely by virtue of charity were the sole heir of its considerable wealth to enter into a marriage that very likely would provide him nothing more than honest affection and feelings of gratitude. I shall not conceal that I would be happy. But it is better that duty make me unhappy than that I would become an ingrate. Let us cease to speak of this. I sense that I have already said more than I should."

Moved by this heartbreaking and yet not unwelcome response, I wished to overcome Julie's inopportune sensitivity. I was just about to open my mouth when Mother came in and immediately began to talk of something else.

For a long time I sought a convenient occasion to make my demands known. Once when Mother was in good humor and was conversing about how I would someday marry, I began to expatiate—as if speaking broadly—on how it debases bonds so sacred to seek a dowry and rich trousseau. I then began to enumerate the qualities I would like to find in a future spouse, subtly defining Julie in the course of so doing. I am not certain whether Mother sensed my ruse, or whether she perceived in my attentions anything more than politeness, or whether Julie's eyes betrayed her, but under the pretext of giving her ward a better education, she decided to send Julie to a nearby convent. In conversation she asked me without pretense if I were not substantially in agreement with her on this matter. A sudden blush betrayed the fact that her question had caught me off guard. Regaining my composure, I began to expostulate broadly on the defects of monastic education. I spoke so eloquently, I daresay, that had Mother not known why I held these convictions, the decision would never have been carried out.

At last the sad day of separation arrived. Only one who has found himself in such a situation will understand what we suffered, the many clandestine tears we shed, the many oaths that were sworn, the declarations we made to each other. After Julie's departure, Mother noticed that deep melancholy had taken possession of me. I avoided the company of others, and my favorite, and almost sole, amusement consisted of visits to the pleasant, now even more precious copse. Afraid that this melancholy would damage my health and wishing to divert me from what she supposed was premature love, she took her brother's advice and decided to send me abroad. M. Damon, once he had won Uncle's approval, greatly expedited my departure so as not to be separated from me. In a matter of a few weeks everything was readied for the trip.

Chapter Six

Just as we were about to set out, unexpected business matters arose, and Mother was forced to dispatch me to one of Poland's finest cities to take care of them. To both my and M. Damon's great regret, the journey abroad was postponed. The city in question was quite far from home, and I was given a letter of introduction to a relative who lived there. Our trip proceeded without incident. I could not locate the persons whom the business concerned; the relative was away and was not expected to return for a whole month.

Since I did not have a single friend in the city, things were rather dull for me until M. Damon mentioned that fortune had put in our path a rather favorable circumstance, for in this very city was a lady of his acquaintance, a baroness de Grankendorff. The baroness, a Pole by birth, had been widowed recently and, having returned from abroad to take possession of a sizable inheritance, had decided to spend a few weeks in the city.

"She receives only trusted friends into her home. After I introduce you there, try not to mention her sojourn here to anyone."

Hastily instructed about how I should behave in company so refined and supplied with a good imagination, I made my entrance, although not without trepidation, onto the stage of the beau monde.

We drove to a rather roomy house where there was a woman ripe in years and her two daughters. After greetings were exchanged and other formalities taken care of, the hostess announced that she was honored to receive so refined a young man. She then presented me to the assembled company, which included four very well-mannered gentlemen. These were friends of M. Damon, I decided, because they conversed with him in hushed tones. What struck me was the bottle of champagne on the table. Around it lay several decks of cards and all the other accoutrements of that trade. One of the four gentlemen wasted little effort prolonging the conversation. He popped the cork and with the foamy wine began to toast the health of the group's new guest. I was unable to restrain myself from toasting the health of our vivacious hostess. Copious toasts to worthy progeny, great success, etc., were proposed one after another. The wine cheered my heart and added eloquence to the utterances that sprang from my lips as I expressed my delight at being in such pleasant company.

The baroness's older daughter seemed most beautiful to me. I was most desirous of striking up a conversation with her but was invited to join in a card game, and thus my emotional outpourings were diverted. Nonetheless, the desire lasted long into the night. The following day I awakened about noon with a strong headache. While I drank tea, M. Damon informed me that I had won no small amount of money as well as the heart of one of those goddesses who had inspired me to be so eloquent the day before. Damon could hardly express adequately his satisfaction with my magnificent bearing. He assured me that I had gained the baroness's esteem and that her older daughter had taken an interest in me that went somewhat beyond the bounds of friendly relations.

We frequented this highly pleasurable house daily. I sensed that the baroness's daughter grew ever fonder of me, but to my great surprise my luck at cards changed. The first two days I went home with a profit, but from then on whenever we played flush, the nines sailed past me, and in matrimony the queen of trumps avoided me. Finally, wanting to recoup in piquet, I was forced to forfeit my aces and, what is worse, my money as well. I lost so much that, had my mother's credit not been good in that city, I would have been forced to return home. My tutor cheered me up in this hour of my distress with the thought that my luck would change. He told how once, playing reversi all night with Cardinal de Fleury, he had lost 160,000 livres. The following day he had won back the money he had lost plus 40,000 more.[11] He further consoled me by adding with a cunning smile that one who finds fortune in love cannot profit from cards. I would have stopped playing without a moment's hesitation had this not posed an obstacle; the baroness's older daughter, who had captivated my heart, liked to amuse herself at cards, and I was a member of her group of players. In addition to my losses, my purse was also depleted by gifts I was obliged to buy for frequent birthdays and name days. It was almost as if they alternated with one another. But not to have presented gifts and hosted feasts on these occasions would have amounted to committing an offense against the lordly thought and feelings M. Damon had recommended.

It was at the end of the fourth week of thus experiencing feelings of the heart that M. Damon at supper, somewhat flushed by wine, quarreled with one of the young men in our group. At first both showed their displeasure rather diplomatically. But one word led to another. Finally M. Damon was called a cheat and a rogue by his adversary. Unable to tolerate this affront to M. le Marquis, I jumped to my feet. The young man drew his sword, and in a flash everyone rose up in arms. There was a great disturbance, and a brawl ensued. We gained the advantage, however, once M. Damon's opponent had received a blow and fallen to the ground. After a long bout, the others fled. Parrying their blows, I found myself in the street surrounded by soldiers and abandoned by everyone. Just as I was thinking of breaking off bayonets, I was wounded in the head—I know not whether by a sword or a battle-ax—and fell senseless on the battlefield.

What happened further I do not remember. I do know that when I opened my eyes, I saw that I was in an unfamiliar place. When I asked where I was, I learned that it was a guardhouse. I immediately asked the soldiers around me to summon their commanding officer. He came immediately and, upon learning my name, sent me at once in his own carriage to my lodgings. Let everyone judge for himself how I felt upon finding myself left with only four bare walls. An astonished landlord gave me the heartbreaking news that the night before my honorable tutor had removed everything and left by post chaise. Moreover, before leaving he had announced that I had departed earlier, on receiving word of my mother's death.

Extremely disconsolate, I made efforts to learn the whereabouts of the runaway Damon, but to no avail. I wanted to inquire after him at the baroness's house, but she was not to be found. It turned out that she was an adventuress who had sojourned but a short time in that city, who deceived and cheated youths by means of her alleged daughters' attractiveness. Doubtless fearing that the consequences of that recent incident in no way boded well for her, she had fled with the booty she had taken from imprudent youths.

Chapter Seven

Mother received news of my adventures sooner than I had expected, or wished. And the letter that I received from her several days later, though it may have lacked the polish of the beau monde, informed me in no uncertain terms that my actions did not meet with her approval. Fearing an unpleasant welcome at home, I wrote letters to various friends and relatives asking them to excuse my rash behavior to Mother and Uncle by saying that it was more the result of ignorance than evidence of a bad character. Parental affection helped me more than the remonstrances of others, particularly after I myself wrote a letter acknowledging my mistakes and promising to change my life completely. The response was favorable. Perhaps it was the desire to see an only child again that helped most, as experience taught me. For after an initial, and overtly chilly, greeting, when Mother took me aside and wanted to deliver with proper dignity the harangue she had prepared, she had difficulty uttering the words. I fell at her feet, which caused her to cry. Moved deeply, I even encouraged her to cry. And in the end, we parted on entirely different terms from those either of us had anticipated; she was even more deeply attached to me than before, and I sincerely wished to improve. Thus I was taught by experience that there is no wickedness so great in a child that it cannot be overcome by parental love.

And so I settled once again at home. Either the fervor of my recent conversion, the memory of an adventure that had caused me embarrassment, or the sight of my exemplary mother effected a miracle. For an entire month I led a model and irreproachable life. M. Damon had taken the romances with him. Since his discourse was still fresh in my mind about French being the sole repository of all knowledge, I did not believe that entertaining or useful Polish books existed or even could exist.

Once in the pantry, where according to time-honored custom I went every day before dinner, sometimes even twice, after having a glass of vodka, to feast on gingerbread sprinkled with sugar, I found in a corner a history of Alexander the Great. Amazed to find in Polish a book that was not religious in nature, I took it back to my room, firmly resolved to read it. That very day I managed to read half a chapter. Alexander's unheard-of adventures amazed me, how he went to sea and how he flew through the air in a cart drawn by griffins. Nevertheless I must confess that I found it difficult to persuade myself to finish the book. I had reached the twentieth chapter—in other words, this heroic undertaking of mine was half complete—when a monk who often stayed in our house discovered what I was reading. He took the book out of my hands and, after scanning several paragraphs, reprimanded me severely for daring to read a work that was both pagan and inspired by Freemasonry. I was frightened by these words and carried the volume back to the pantry. When Mother was informed of this evil, she had the book burned.

Among the many neighbors who visited us frequently was the local pantler's wife, one of Mother's close relatives. At one time she had been at the royal court; more important, she had once been to the Diet in Warsaw. Usually, not long after arriving, she would launch into a discourse about the splendors of Warsaw, about various scandals of her time, about good breeding in ladies, *gallants hommes,* and exquisite feelings in both sexes. These conversations enabled her to dominate the whole neighborhood. In church no one dared to occupy the pew in front of her. In feast day processions she walked right behind the priest. When our vicar distributed Christmas gifts, he always named and honored her first. And although this partiality would greatly irritate parishioners, her standing was so well established that even the cup-bearer's old wife, at one time first lady in the entire area, patiently bore what amounted to a personal insult. Once the pantler's wife, discoursing about the reading of books, told those present that, while she was in Warsaw, both men and women of quality were perusing *The Faithful Calloandro*.[12] When I asked whether that gallant, like my Alexander, flew through the air and fought the whole world, she said: "You are wrong, sir, if you think that on the basis of such things one is deemed a first-rate gallant. Calloandro, although courageous in many of his encounters, was not esteemed for his courage. As his epithet clearly indicates, his inviolate goodwill toward the one he loved dearly, the genuine and heroic services he rendered her even at great risk to life and limb, and the abiding constancy of his spirited feelings is what made him worthy of the appellation 'Faithful.' That appellation is more splendid than all of those that honor the knights and monarchs of the world. Do not forget, sir, that to be faithful to one's beloved is to be at once great, splendid, courageous, and just."

I had no answer to such a response. I remembered, however, that romance about Cyrus that my tutor had brought to my attention, and after dinner, when the guests had begun to depart, I asked her if she would care to lend me the Polish version of this choice work. At first she fretted about this. When finally in tears I insisted, she condescended to grant my request, and that very evening the much-desired *Calloandro* entered our house.

Chapter Eight

Mother had not yet learned that a number of creditors held notes for substantial sums bearing my signature, sums of which M. Damon and his entourage had availed themselves. At first I did not dare bring up the matter. I soon became fearful, however, lest the creditors make direct appeals to her, and at an opportune moment confessed everything outright. She absolved but did not spare me. She ordered that the creditors be notified to present their notes, with the understanding that each would be given his due. To be sure, she could have refused to pay off the creditors, and indeed this was the advice of her business agent. Her conscience, however, did not permit her to ignore people who had been harmed thanks to the transgressions of another. So, either not knowing how to draw distinctions between matters that were legal and those that were just or not wishing to, she preferred to encroach upon what wealth she possessed than to encroach upon the poor. I can safely say *poor* because those in question were merchants and tradesmen of our provincial capital.

The reading of *The Faithful Calloandro* stirred imperceptibly in me the desire to further the education of feeling begun by M. Damon. The country seemed too limited an arena for practicing the precepts I had so avidly learned. Julie was not there. I discovered that the object of my affections was the daughter of the subvoivode. When I began to make advances, however, the subvoivode approached me in anticipation, promising his daughter, asking my terms, and stipulating joint tenancy of the property involved. Such barbarity perturbed me greatly. Thoroughly disgusted with life in the country, I prevailed upon Mother to dispatch me to Warsaw, which she did in the company of an uncle who was to represent our province in the Diet.

Every young man from the country arriving for the first time in the capital city finds himself overcome by the great variety of sights that unfold before his eyes. That impression was even more intense in me because I so longed to see and get to know (as they say nowadays) the beau monde. When I compared my clumsiness with the marvelous dash of the Warsaw gallants, I at first felt great shame and humiliation. Uncle's instructions and explanations helped me to acquire the proper social graces and bearing, but it was the ladies who proved to be my real teachers. Thanks to their attentions I rid myself of the vice of modesty, so inappropriate to the gallant's calling. Made fun of in polite society for blushing shamefully, I became daring. I grew to learn that what ordinary people call slander, polite society considers amusing banter, the essence of polite conversation. I soon became so adept at this that I outdid those I had earlier been told to imitate.

I had convinced myself that my refinement was in no way lacking, when an outspoken friend of two days disabused me of this notion. The friend had come to Warsaw in a cheap coat and without a servant but now was traveling in an English carriage with springs and axles bending under the weight of amply built haiduks.[13] He took a liking to me and invited me for oysters. After the other guests left, he began to talk.

"I know that you will not take umbrage if I give you certain advice and prescribe certain rules to you as one who has recently debuted on this great stage, advice and rules that, as you can see from my circumstances, I have followed to my advantage. If one were able to exercise control over one's own birth, undoubtedly I would have chosen your station or one even better. But with me things were different. To be sure, I was born a nobleman, but one so poor that my parents, who thought solely about providing for the family, had no time to think about my education. As soon as I had reached the age of eleven, I was sent out—actually pushed out—of the nest. Besides a blessing, I was given nothing for the journey. I found employment, and a certain natural zest endeared me to those for whom I worked. I realized that this zest with some dash added would serve to bring me happiness. I preserved and cultivated this natural gift as best I could. Over time I augmented and perfected it to such a degree that it developed gradually into insolence. He who wishes to accomplish something in this world must be brazen-faced.

"Why is it, I ask you, that people who are virtuous, upright, handsome, and learned complain of their fate? They suffer for the sole reason that they know not how to sell their wares. Do they suppose that modesty enhances virtue? That is absolute nonsense. Those times when virtue was sought have long passed; they probably never existed at all (which I strongly suspect). One must forego virtue in the name of happiness or ponder the vanities of this world on an empty stomach. It is good and most desirable to possess talents, but it is more of an achievement if, having no talents whatsoever, you pass for being accomplished. I will not entertain you with my adventures. You may surmise that they have been both many and varied for me to have acquired the standing you now see me enjoying. I will thus proceed to describe the various methods one must use to gain favor and to develop the reputation of a gallant.

"First of all, one must acquire, to as great an extent as possible, the threefold reputation of *gallant homme,* blade, and philosopher. The third quality, though not necessary in the past, is now essential. The fashionable young man of today is quite different from the gallants of Louis XIV's France or August II's Poland. The expression of feeling at that time was so prescribed by decorum, modesty, and mystery that a lover who had chosen an object for his love either took the narrow path of holy matrimony or remained to the end of his days a near slave to the one he loved. The smallest infringement of the rules of gallantry was regarded as an unforgivable transgression. Ladies and gentlemen, martyrs to convention, sometimes thought that they sincerely loved one another when in fact they found one another's company boring.

"The ladies perceived the glaring shortcomings of all this and, being bolder than we men, cast off the inconvenient yoke of decorum. 'The longer lovebirds weep, the worse their plight,' said a well-bred and very fashionable lady to me recently.[14] Staidness is now the attribute of provincial minds alone. Possibly in the country people still fall in love in the traditional manner. With us here in Warsaw, even in market stalls and workshops a mania for gallantry is now the prevailing fashion. Consequently, it is considered passé to dwell on the emotions, to sigh, to cry, to wait patiently.

"You should impress people with your insolence, dramatic gestures, bold speech, slander; take pride in imagined happiness, stylish dress, elegant English carriage, extravagant expenditures. When you are at a social gathering among ladies, have a page bring you notes one after another that you have composed yourself. Read them as if absent-mindedly, all the while complaining that you cannot find a free moment for yourself. When asked from whom these messages and notes come, say—now with an ingenuous air, now with a smile—that it is a personal matter, of little import, etc. Should there be a fire in the fireplace, go over to it and, after beginning another conversation, throw a note into the flames so subtly and circumspectly that everyone notices.

"Your popularity in social circles will also be enhanced if you casually drop names in the course of ordinary conversation: 'I was at the hetman's,' 'I played with the chancellor,' 'Went hunting with the voivode,' etc. This style is somewhat akin to the art of swagger. And to gain recognition as a swaggerer, one must become familiar with those who by means of bloodless duels have earned the reputation of being courageous knights. Recounting bold acts and reckless deeds in the company of ladies or serious-minded people can help a great deal in many situations. Once you have gone abroad, a wider field of this kind of activity will be opened to you, for you will not have to fear witnesses. Thus you will be able to flaunt your courage even before swaggerers. It also would not be ill advised to have at all times next to your bed a pair of pistols, even if they are not loaded, and in the same chamber hang or place in the corner a sword with a cross guard.

"As to philosophy, you should know that our present age is one of enlightenment. Along with English frock coats, philosophy has come into vogue. In the boudoirs of the most fashionable ladies, right next to embroidery hoops and face powder you will find volumes of M. Rousseau, the philosophical works of Voltaire, and other writings of that sort. Consequently, it is absolutely necessary to prove you can carry on a discussion about such matters should someone turn to you with a question. Do not think, however, that for this reason you must constantly read to improve your mind or enter the realm of profound speculation. It is not nearly so difficult to become a philosopher as you may think. Praise only what others criticize, think whatever you wish as long as you take pains to be incisive now and again, jest at the expense of religion, make bold resolutions, and talk loudly. I guarantee that in no time you will pass for a great philosopher..."

He intended to say more, but word came that it was time for him to be on his way. Thus regretfully our discussion ended, and we set off together for a soiree.

Chapter Nine

Not long after this conversation I received word of my mother's death. It was only natural that I should feel satisfaction at the prospect of gaining my freedom. Notwithstanding this, I was genuinely grieved by the loss. Time healed my sorrow, and various plans began to take shape in my imagination. Travel to foreign lands proved the most exciting. Without leaving Warsaw, I made all the arrangements and preparations for such a journey. My new mentor put together an itinerary for my future peregrinations. I noted that in the midst of helping me, he seemed somewhat distracted. He confessed that because of certain very urgent business he was forced to seek a loan of five hundred ducats. I at once offered to help him and, wanting to display my magnanimity, counted out a thousand ducats without demanding a promissory note or interest.

Once I appeared in deep mourning, I seemed to attract others' hearts, for I was included in the company of the capital's most fashionable gallants. And the ladies also began to regard me more favorably. There was a round of dinners and soirees. Mr. Nicholas Wisdom was the life of every gathering. When I received the money Mother had left me, half of it was consumed by faro and quinze,[15] the remainder by merchants and tradesmen.

My friend had recommended that I take with me on my journey several thousand ducats in cash as well as a banker's draft for several thousand more. Not wishing to delay my departure, I wrote to my plenipotentiary, instructing him to mortgage one or two of my villages at the Lvovian Exchanges[16] and bring the money as quickly as possible to Warsaw. He carried out my bidding with even greater zeal than I had anticipated. Instead of mortgaging two villages, he mortgaged three and came to Warsaw bearing coins of the purest gold obtainable. The speed with which he delivered the money so impressed me that I made him agree not only to look after my business in my absence but to administer all my property as well. He accepted this commission with great reluctance, arguing that this would amount to an act of heroism since he very likely would make himself an object of people's slander, would run afoul of my relatives, would expose himself to personal loss, etc. To help him overcome his qualms and to demonstrate that I understood how serious his commitment was, I advanced him several thousand zloty, placing a lien for that amount against a small village. Only when I was satisfied that my affairs would be well handled in my absence did I begin to think seriously about my forthcoming trip.

Half my wardrobe was already packed when I received a letter from my plenipotentiary informing me that my presence was required in Lublin because of a lawsuit occasioned by my precipitous expulsion of a neighbor from a small village. By rights the village should have been part of my inheritance thanks to my family's very ancient claims to it. I turned to a trusted friend for advice. It was decided that I should go, obtaining beforehand letters of intro-duction to the deputies in Lublin.[17] I therefore made visits to several lords, gaining from them these coveted passports to justice.

One of the lords, to whom I had lost three hundred ducats at quinze the very night before, promised his help most eagerly and invited me to his place for supper. Seated at the card table I felt duty-bound to demonstrate my gratitude and was so artful in my deliberate effort to lose that, before I had awoken in the forenoon of the following day, letters of reference *volanti sigillo* had been delivered.[18] On each there was a *postscriptum* in the patron's own hand. Recently I came across one of those letters (I do not know why it was never used). It is presented here for the edification of any of my readers who finds himself in like circumstances:

To the Most Honorable N.N.
My Highly Honored Lord and Peer!

   Your Lordship's most salutary and refined feelings, evident in every circumstance but even more so in that circumstance whereby the fatherland entrusted to your solicitous care the administration of sacred justice, are known to me. *Sitiens justitiam,* Mr. Wisdom, a gentleman for whom I have affection, prays that Your Honor oblige him with your patronage.[19] Being cognizant of that friendship with which you have honored me for so long, he asks that I make petition on his behalf. If, Most Honorable Sire, you deign to succor him with your effectual favor, it will be a sign of your continued goodwill toward me and prompt me to fulfill efficaciously those obligations that have been respectfully bestowed upon me.

Your Honor's Sincerely Well-Wishing Peer and Humble Servant,

N.N.

P.S Most sincere and beloved friend, be kind to the one herein recommended
and do not fail to remember the recommender.

Chapter Ten

With my arrival in Lublin new vistas were opened to me.[20] I became
acquainted with my affairs from a totally different perspective, one
previously unknown to me. My plenipotentiary began to instruct
me about what I would have to do in order to conduct business
successfully here. In this respect my Warsaw *oraculum* was unable
to enlighten me much because, having neither inheritance nor
money from property loans, he lacked altogether experience in legal
maneuvering and thus was not in a position to be familiar with or
understand the proceedings at Lublin and Piotrków.[21] Subsequently, I learned that in order to win a case one must, first, have
his own collateral or enjoy the support of powerful patrons; second,
be acquainted with, a friend of, or related to the judges, or, if this
is lacking, possess that which, though I dare not give its name, will,
however, in time of need prove to be either equal to or greater
than friendship and kinship. The apparent justice of a case counts
for very little.

So instructed, I began a series of visits to each individual judge
with a generous supply of reference letters in hand. Many a time I
had to precede the sunrise, climb up dark and incommodious stairs
to a second, third, or even fourth floor, and wait in a dark anteroom
with a humble throng of fellow petitioners for that blissful moment
when His Benevolence would awake or deign to receive us. The
door of the master's chamber would be opened by a Matthias or
an Ivan, a faithful Catholic recently turned Muslim by His Honor
for the court public.[22] Once admitted to the chamber, I had the
honor of seeing a judge awesome in all respects. Without stirring
from his chair, he would hear out my humble petition. He would

measure me several times from head to foot with a lordly and severe eye and then order his valet to bring a beautiful, elegant, old-fashioned basin on which was etched (I noticed) someone else's coat of arms. Only when he had finished washing properly would he dismiss me, saying with a terseness characteristic of high ministers: "I will see what this is about. You will have a decision in due time."

To this day I can still picture the house of one of my judges. From the way in which his official apartments—once a chamber with an alcove, now an audience chamber and study—were appointed, one sensed a curious rivalry between magnificence and indigence. The chamber's walls were covered with hangings, one a flaming gore of threadbare satinet, another of checkered crewel. A large table stood in the middle covered by a costly Persian rug, and around the chamber were positioned various common wooden stools and an old armchair upholstered in golden leather. The walls of the narrow bedroom were bare. Next to the bed was a small screen, and instead of a bed curtain there was a threadbare blanket. The bed itself was narrow, and over it shone a tapestry of samite. Watches set with precious stones hung in a row, as did gorgeous caparisons, gold swords, and cutlasses. Astounded by this unexpected splendor, I thought to myself: "Oh, how prosperous must this city be that such beautiful objects can be obtained so easily and for so little money!"

I proceeded to make more and more official visits. I was resting at home, exhausted from this disagreeable traveling about, when my plenipotentiary came to me in haste to report that tomorrow would be the name day of a very important judge and that therefore it was necessary to prepare gifts worthy of so eminent a person. His Honor, John the Evangelist in Piotrków, had now become in Lublin, John the Baptist.[23] *In gratiam* of the great festivity, my adversary was giving a ball. So as not to capitulate to him but to outshine his generosity, I ordered my French carriage with fancy gilt harness moved immediately to the coach house of the name day celebrant. And not without result. For on the following day I sensed a sign of his favor. While climbing the steps of the city hall, he leaned on me, and I had the honor of helping him reach the very courtroom.

After these steps were taken, my plenipotentiary and I held council about how to begin the suit, how to conduct it, and what would be the best possible way to assure a favorable outcome. And since my plenipotentiary himself had caused all this, because it was he who had prompted me to chase a nobleman out of the village and that in turn had produced several murders and a gash on my adversary's head, I anticipated that the opinions he expressed would be straightforward and that he would support the suit wholeheartedly once it was begun. When we closeted ourselves for a tête-à-tête, he spoke as follows:

"My long training, the importance of this matter, and my sincere affection for you as my benefactor require that I give you good counsel. And so, with the fewest possible words, I will proceed to the heart of the matter. First of all, we must engage nearly the entire *palestra*.[24] Although according to the provisions of the law code they may not all become involved—only three can plead any one case—now and then cases have been divided into categories.[25] For each category we will need to engage separate defense counsels and still others to present the counterarguments. Those remaining we will call to a meeting so that they cannot be approached afterward by the opposing side. And thus our adversary will find no one to come to his defense but the dregs, who are not as well known by the court and who can easily be intimidated.

"I know several of the most celebrated jurists who are on the most friendly terms with the deputies. They are accustomed to charming these deputies for clients in ways known to them alone, as you must understand. Excellent theologians, they know how to adjudicate scruples, to neutralize doubt, to render alarming situations harmless, to interpret law. Armed with information about the most intimate facts, they wield authority over those whose reason, conscience, and needs they comprehend best. We must therefore ingratiate ourselves with them to as great a degree as we can.

"I am also acquainted with several persons in the *palestra* who know how to read the old orthography of ancient and obscure records. Though sometimes half of an official document may have rotted away or been gnawed on by mice, they read it again and again and copy out excerpts. And the officials who must authenticate, sign, and seal the sections copied refuse to verify the work out of respect for the copyists' abilities, blindly approving excerpts the latter submit. So I will fetch you one I know well who more than once has proved to be reliable. I will relate our case to him and tell him what documents we still require, and I assure you that he will find them for us. But such a search will be costly. And having done this, we must then attempt to win over the deputy who keeps the Book of Judgments.[26] You can't imagine how necessary this item is to our case."

I hugged and kissed heartily this solicitous and benevolent plenipotentiary of mine. Taking steps to fulfill his helpful advice, I made him agree to invite as many lawyers as he saw fit to a meeting at my quarters. In the meantime I began to make preparations for the meeting. Twelve large, gallon-sized flagons of wine were brought, each costing six ducats. Next to them I put out sheets of good paper, "summaries,"[27] and scratch paper on a small table for recording information and for noting the content of records.

Chapter Eleven

Before long ten serious and stately lawyers paid me a visit. More than half were acquainted with my case thanks to previous conferences held elsewhere. I had to exchange formal courtesies with each of them. Several flagons of wine were placed on the table. My plenipotentiary then came over and asked to speak to me. Taking me aside, he turned his face so that the others could not see it and whispered into my ear: "Take heed, sir, of the gentleman in the parrot-green *kontusz*[28] belted at the chest…"

"I see him," I said.

"Well, that gentleman is on good terms with the Most Honorable *N.N.* Thanks to him *N.N.* not long ago was given a village for life by Voivode *N.N.* after a suit was won. But that is a strict secret. Now that other gentleman, the one wearing the damascened scimitar with golden inlay and an ivory handle, got the scimitar as a gift from Deputy *N.N.* for procuring a gratis three-year lease. Then, there is a gentleman with a little moustache cut à la Charles XII who is advanced in years, wearing an old, black, and threadbare *kontusz*. He normally writes up verdicts for the deputy who keeps the Book of Judgments in those cases where the scribe has agreed to relinquish this duty. We must be mindful of him as well."

Returning to those assembled, I drank to the good health of the honorable *palestra* and to the bonds of friendship. The oldest gentleman drank to my health in return, and having tasted the wine and declared it both first-rate and properly aged, he proposed a toast to unending good fortune, that it might be visited on everyone present. While additional glasses were being drained, one of the more assiduous gentlemen of the group said to me: "Honored Sir! One occupation need not encumber another. Time marches on. Let us acquaint ourselves with the suit. If we find something lacking during the reading of the records, a glass will nicely do the trick."

"Agreed! Agreed!" the others chimed in. Everyone sat down around the little table in accordance with his respective area of expertise.

My plenipotentiary began to give them information about the case. Each of the lawyers jotted down the most essential facts. There were interruptions, records were examined, and prior judgments were quoted. All of this interfered not a little with the presentation, prolonging it considerably.

We were already halfway through the record when an elegantly dressed young man noisily entered the room. In tow was his Cossack groom with a pigtail braided with red ribbon and his valet, dressed in green, with a hunting knife, who seemed to represent a court guard. They were preceded by a young and frisky pointer that, evidently sensing that there was eating going on at the table, quickly clambered up on it and overturned a large goblet filled with wine. All my papers and the notes of the defense counsels were drenched. Worse still, several beautiful *kontuszes* and *zhupans*[29] were stained with wine. Everyone jumped up from the table, and one whose clothing had been stained said: "Respected kin of the treasurer! You should know that I am going to complain to your most honorable uncle about the damage I have suffered."

My plenipotentiary quickly whispered into my ear that I should receive this young man with utmost civility, for he was the president's own nephew and supposedly had been promised the command of a cavalry detachment.[30] It was his wont, or rather assignment, to receive training in law by attending meetings of this sort, and his mentor was the defense counsel wearing the bright red doublet. The latter would bring him to meetings of the well-to-do, who, in turn, recognized that they should be grateful for the honor. Consequently, I welcomed the young man with compliments appropriate to so desirable a guest. I then offered a toast to the health of his most honorable uncle. This was repeated several times with a mere change in title. Afterward, with the permission of our guest, who demanded to listen as well, we sat down and continued to review the information about the case. It must be admitted that the young man paid more attention to his dog than to the details of the case. He whistled, ordered the dog to lie down and to fetch a cap that was tossed. Although this was a nuisance to those listening, we praised the dog and its master, at the same time finishing the review.

Copious goblets of wine provided a respite. Suddenly, one of the lawyers turned to me and said: "We have an adequate understanding of the case. It has two facets. It is simultaneously *juris et facti,* that is, legal and actual. As regards the legality of driving out the nobleman, beating and detaining him, and slaying his servants, you should know that this same nobleman has had you summoned to appear before the Expulsionum Registry, the registry I judge proper to this suit.[31] So, if that registry favors the nobleman's petition, the court will not examine the case *in causam juris,*[32] for the law prevents it from doing so; instead it will order that the nobleman be reinstated and you punished with fines and time in the tower. On the other hand, as for *ad causam juris* in a case such as this, when you present your rights to the hamlet and summon the nobleman to appear before the Provincial Registry where you have formally applied to have the case adjudicated, you may be confident that the presiding jurists will favor you, should you allow the case to be decided here.[33]

"If yours, that is, the petitioner's, inheritance of this hamlet is confirmed, it can then be anticipated that by dint of this ruling, the factual side of the case will collapse. The use of force will not be acknowledged, and income will be exacted from your adversary for the time he used the land. He will have to compensate for the damage done, and to estimate this a tour of inspection will be arranged by the court. If, on the other hand, you have no faith in the local court, then as a minimum you should request that the case be sent on to the municipal court,[34] in which you have greater faith, or a tour of inspection should be arranged by court officials you yourself designate.

"You then will be forced to worry lest the case find itself in the Expulsionum Registry, something for which the opposing side will strive. Thus, it will be necessary to ingratiate yourself with the deputies so that they do their best not to promote this registry and have the case, when considered on Wednesday, postponed to Thursday and made to proceed at a snail's pace. On the other hand, let them press forward with the Provincial Registry. Let as many court proceedings as possible be sent on to municipalities for tours of inspection. In some instances permit the defense to agree with the prosecution insofar as it is possible. The remainder shall then be dropped *per non sunt* by grace of the president's bell.[35] In this way the three hundred registry applications that preceded yours will simply melt away. Beg the honorable treasurer's son to put in a good word for you with his uncle, and I assure you that you will get his support in any form you specify."

He finished, and everyone said that they could add nothing to so splendid and so excellent an opinion. Everyone moved away from the little table. I meanwhile invited the treasurer's son into another room. Knowing that he was a hunter, I took down a rifle and a pair of French pistols from a peg on the wall and presented them to him, asking that he be my intermediary in winning the favor of his most honorable uncle.

The lawyers meanwhile collected their fees, those who stood to lose something in the proceedings receiving double fees. Then they went back to their homes or on to other meetings. I accompanied the treasurer's son out to the street, commending myself to his good graces.

Chapter Twelve

Back in my lodgings I began talking with my plenipotentiary about the first stage of the case, now safely under way. He praised my *activitatem*. To the counsel he had given earlier he added that one of the lawyers at the meeting had told him we should obtain an old document proving that the nobleman's parcel of land could be seized by me, because for a very long time it had been part of an adjacent village that I owned.

"I said that we already had such," continued my plenipotentiary. "Consequently, I must now go call on one of my friends who possesses the secret of deciphering, writing, and, if necessary, composing documents in the ancient orthography. I will tell him exactly what we need, and he will 'find' precisely that."

In an hour my plenipotentiary returned with a cheerful face and announced that he had been able to order that which we needed. Everything would be ready in three days.

"Such records," he said, "are not only useful to our suit, but embellish it. A moldy and worm-eaten scrap of parchment has the stamp of antiquity and a dignity that will mask obvious flaws."

The third day arrived, the day appointed for delivery of the parchment records. Our learned calligrapher turned up. He told me what my plenipotentiary had instructed him to search out and then drew from under his jacket three extracts, which he assured me were real treasures. They would serve as peremptory pleas given in response to the opposing side's rejoinders and would bring me victory. Heartened by a promise so attractive, I impatiently opened and examined them. The following is what I found.

The first extract contained the *oblata*[36] of privilege on parchment of the Ruthenian prince Vasili Davidovich, who had granted to the Yatvyag nobleman Zejmund Łopata,[37] Pig's Corner Range, which lay within the boundaries of Szumin, a village that the above-mentioned Zejmund had inherited. The second extract, written a hundred years later, contained a legal "view"[38] of the boundary between *praedium militare alias,*[39] the farm incorporated within the village of Szumin that lies at one end of the woods called Pig's Corner, and the prince's village of Paprzyca. The third extract, dated 163 years later, contained a description of how the land inherited by my great-great-grandfather and his brothers was apportioned among them in accordance with which my forebear was given the village of Szumin (which I possess to this day), whereas Nadlesny Grange (clearly its original name had been changed) was given to his brother Szczesny. Two other brothers divided the inherited money. The sisters *abrenunciarunt*.[40]

My expert searcher departed, not without receiving expressions of gratitude and abundant recompense. Then one of the sympathetic deputies abetting me arrived. Taking me aside (for I had guests), he said: "Our whole plan and our willingness to serve you could fail tomorrow unless you act to prevent this. No matter what happens, the case we are now adjudicating will last until six o'clock and no longer. After six, according to law, we must use the Tapping Registry.[41] As I have learned, no cases are to be introduced that would keep us occupied all day tomorrow. So tomorrow for certain, as on a Thursday, in accordance with the statute,[42] the Expulsionum Registry must be brought forward, and your case is third on it. I know from the defense counsel that the first two cases will be dropped *per non sunt*. Consequently, there is reason to be most fearful here. None of your friends will be able to find ways to save you if it is proved that you committed an act of expulsion and you yourself cannot deny such. There will then be an order to revise the entire case, and according to the terms of the law, you will be penalized. Accordingly, I do not see any other alternative but to abort the session for the whole day first thing in the morning.[43]

"There are eight sitting lay deputies to deal with here. Consequently, we must make three disappear without fail. The Honorable N.N. you will invite to a hunt taking place three miles from here. Tell him you know there is a bear to be had, and he will fly after it with pleasure. To the Honorable X.X. you will give one hundred ducats, without any ceremony, so that he will take off for the fair at Leczna. I myself will be ill all day."

Everything happened according to our scheme. We aborted the session successfully, my adversary despaired, and I escaped the tower and fines.

Having thus dealt with the Thursday peril, I petitioned their honors to make up for the lost day by expediting the Provincial

Registry. There were 232 cases ahead of mine on it. And indeed, on Friday 60 were dropped, on Saturday 80, and on Monday the rest. On the evening of the same day a brief for my case was filed.

When I returned to my lodgings that night, my stableman told me that the deputy who had gone hunting with me had asked if I would sell him the carriage in which we had ridden. The soft ride pleased him. He made the stableman promise to relay my decision the following day because he intended to send home for a coach, and were he to get my carriage, it would save him money (he was greatly burdened by court costs). The request threw me into confusion because I had only this one coach left. But after thinking it over and in view of the fact that the case was already being adjudicated, I decided to make him a present of the carriage and instructed my stableman to ask for nothing in return, simply to beg the deputy to show me his kindness. Nor was he to suppose—God forbid—that I was tempting his conscience by means of this bagatelle. The deputy was quite pleased with the present, and even more so by the fact that I did not view this gift as a bribe and was dealing so delicately with his conscience.

The next day, when their honors sat to further consider my case, the opposing side introduced four accessories,[44] asking (as was customary) that the relation of judges and litigants to the case be verified. Each time there were recesses—some long, some short, but all favorable to me. Later one of the deputies told me that they gave particular consideration to the problem of how to make certain that the nobleman did not leave Lublin when they imposed fines on him. So my opponent lost all the accessories, and an *inducant negotium* order was issued.[45]

My adversary foresaw that he was likely to lose the case and was ready, in order to avoid further appearances in court, to accept the verdict in absentia. However, his attorney, whom I had won over, whispered in his ear that large fines would be imposed on him *pro temerario recessu et extenuatione temporis.*[46] Knowing no Latin, my adversary was frightened by these mellifluous phrases and, willy-nilly, like a wolf in the pit, bit the bait.

Since I was the plaintiff on this registry, the lawyer best qualified by virtue of force and volume of speech introduced the case. After the clerk had cried out "Silence!" he spoke as follows:

"While the power of the wealthy seems to stifle the laws, to disturb public tranquillity, and to threaten the sense of equality among the country's gentry, anyone closely considering the forfeiture of this power must admit that the weak are made stronger as the intensity of the power of the wealthy weakens and wastes away. To express this more clearly, the boldness that the possession of riches permits grows weak and declines as those riches are spent. On the other hand, we find that the impudence of the poorer citizen is readily inflamed, that the example of profits reaped by others encourages him to achieve the same, that penury does not make him attentive to the common good, to order, justice, and the law. The hope of vile profits is the only thing he takes into consideration. Losses do not discourage him, for accustomed to deprivation, he takes great risks. He has nothing to lose in risking his life, and even if he endangers his health, his lot in life may improve.

"Honorable members of this supreme tribunal, in this dignified Areopagus stands Mr. Wisdom with a complaint about the impudent attack of a neighbor. In this highest court he seeks a stronghold to fortify his rights to the property that has belonged to his family for five centuries. *Victrix causa diis placuit, sed victa Catoni.*[47] Indeed, Honorable Marshal and President and Most Honorable Luminaries of Poland, *ingens gloria Dardanorum:*[48] he stands boldly, for he is innocent; he stands covetously, for *sitiens justitam;* he stands resignedly, for *impavidum ferient ruinae.*"[49]

I omit further exposition of the case. When the famous privilege of Prince Vasili granting the range to Zejmund Łopata, the Yatvyag, was elaborated, the judges marveled at a document of such antiquity. I overheard one judge ask another, who enjoyed the reputation of being a learned person, what was meant by Yatvyags, whether they were some ancient family or people. To which the sage earnestly replied: "Honorable Sir, the Yatvyags were what the Arian or Jansenist heretics are now. Banished by law, they left Poland; God be praised, that they are no longer in our midst."

His Honor the reverend president listened to this and opined:

"My Honorable *N.N.,* this is not how it was. According to Duń-czewski,[50] the Yatvyags conducted war in Poland, that is, they stirred up rebellions, and then formed alliances. The Łopatas must therefore have been a prominent family, like the Chmielnickis."

The Honorable *N.N.* took a stand against the president's criticism. Both sides defended their opinions with increasing passion. Unable to bear such effrontery any longer, the reverend president called for a recess. The recess lasted more than two hours, after which it was announced that the trial would resume the following day.

Chapter Thirteen

When we assembled the following day at the town hall, news spread that my opponent had surmised what would happen and had fled Lublin during the night, saying nothing to anyone. No defense attorney appeared at the town hall to represent him. Someone was sent to his lodgings, and the news was confirmed by his landlord. We were all quite confused. Their Honors regretted the damage to the coffer;[51] and consequently, an *in contumaciam* decree was issued,[52] a triumph for me. On the other hand, to show my gratitude I was obliged to pay *salva repetitione* in lieu of a fine.[53]

In the wake of the felicitous end to the suit, my plenipotentiary asked me what I thought about the wit and eloquence of lawyers. I in return asked him from what source lawyers drew their eloquence, learning, and knowledge and where were the schools at which the successors of Cicero received their training. For I had learned that this was supposedly a distinct realm of learning, one both strenuous and requiring great diligence.

My plenipotentiary laughed and said, "There are no schools for defense attorneys in Poland. Everyone goes through the paces that I, for example, went through. After I finished school, my father, not having the means to present me at court, entrusted me to the city chancery. There I was told to write out extracts of official records as well as formal complaints, reports on visits to scenes of crimes, summonses, contracts, and so forth.[54] After cramming my brain with forms for three years, the *susceptant*[55] finally assigned me the task of composing a formal complaint on the basis of submitted materials. Many a try was torn up before I received his approval. My dear sir, no mean mind is needed for the composition of a complaint, since it must be done *cum boris, gais et graniciebus.*[56] After spending two years as an apprentice in the chancery, I had only just begun to comprehend the *formalitatem.*[57]

"After this Father sent me to the court *palestra* for additional training. I was first a 'dependent,' then later an 'agent' with a lawyer.[58] It was my duty to make accurate inventories of record 'summaries' of cases that the lawyer took on, to learn the summaries, should explanation be necessary in the course of the trial, to go to meetings with the lawyer, take official papers to the city hall, and sometimes take bottles to the lawyer at his lodgings. After some six years the lawyer, presumably conscious of the physicians' maxim, *faciamus experimentum in anima vili,*[59] ordered me to enter pleas in a case brought by an indigent nobleman. I spent several days in preparation. When the time came to enter the plea, however, I began to speak in a trembling voice. I got my words so mixed up that the judges burst out laughing, and the nobleman was in tears. I was hardly able to enunciate the final arguments.

"By the grace of God, and despite my want of eloquence, the poor devil won his petty case. In time, growing bolder, I began to ingratiate myself with younger people, especially those who were members of the aristocracy. I entered into lucrative negotiations on the strength of their names. Sometimes I had to deliver their notes, at other times even more than notes. Finally, aided by the patronage of a certain aristocratic lady who was influential in the courts, I became a lawyer, her plenipotentiary, and in the course of time, yours, too, my benefactor."

Having paid the deputy who had charge of the Book of Judgments for the decision decree as well as the scribe who had misused his pen for my sake, I found myself completely out of money and things of value. Having lost more than half of the amount I had borrowed to go abroad and weary from weeks of inconvenience, I borrowed a carriage from a Dominican prior (since I no longer had one of my own) and returned to Warsaw with a fever that recurred every three days.

It was necessary to make entirely new preparations for travel abroad. The neighboring nobleman did not want to give back Nadlesny Grange, which had been awarded to me, and, counting on better luck in a future year, had a complaint *de noviter repertis documentis* issued.[60] As the time for obtaining mortgages had passed, there was nowhere to borrow money. It was therefore necessary for me to pay a visit to a man most obliging under such circumstances. I pawned to him my silver and jewelry, paying a 12 percent commission in advance [61] and retaining the right to redeem this pledge in a year or forfeit it. He gave me two thousand "Polish" ducats in cash, calculated at the rate of sixteen zloty, twenty-two and a half groszy to the ducat. Since Polish money could not be used abroad, I went back to him to request that he exchange the ducats for gold. He agreed to work out the transaction with a friend, despite the great difficulty of obtaining gold. I daresay the friend was his own pouch. The next day the man came to me to say that the friend would only exchange ducats at a rate of eighteen zloty per gold piece. I permitted myself to take this obvious loss and, receiving the money, put such energy into preparation for the journey that within ten days, having made my farewell visits and given my plenipotentiary general instructions, to my great joy I was able to set out.

A brief diary containing some observations I made at the time follows. I present them here because I believe them to be of interest.

Chapter Fourteen

Diary of the Trip to Paris

I left Warsaw at 9:00 A.M., the twentieth of November, taking the stage that runs to Vienna via Kraków. I rode in a silver-coated Berlin carriage for two with seats upholstered in yellow velvet. My valet, La Rose, rode with me. On the box sat Michael, the footman, and Christian, the cook.

On the very first day not far from the city of Nadarzyn, I ordered that a Jew be beaten for not coming to a halt by a dam when he heard the postilions' trumpets.

In Drzewica[62] I bought beautiful material for five waistcoats and a ready-made set of passementeries to trim my servants' livery. They would come in handy in Paris.

The remainder of the trip to Kraków was uneventful. I had to get out several times when we crossed bridges. One bridge even collapsed under the weight of the carriage. Fortunately, the stream under it was not very deep. And as I learned, the merchants do pay tolls there.

I alighted in Kraków on the night of the twenty-seventh because the roads were in very bad condition. A vast city and a beautiful one. It is indeed evident that this was once the capital of the Polish kingdom. I viewed with interest the remarkable sights of the city and surrounding area: Queen Wanda's grave, the sorcerer Twardowski's school, the academy. *NB:* The wine here is both cheap and good, but it seems to me that the kegs are smaller than they used to be.

I left Kraków on December 2, and the very next day, though not without regret, I departed Poland. The first city in Silesia is Bilsk.[63] To reach Moravia required several stage changes in Silesia. The roads are superior to ours. In some of the inns the beer is good, though too heady. It does not measure up to that from Wilanów, Inflanty, and Bielawa. Olomouc is a fairly sizable and solid city.[64] It is the first fortress I have seen.

On the tenth of December at 10:30 I reached Vienna. My belongings were examined and shaken unmercifully. I had to wait half a day in my lodgings for my luggage. In the meantime, since I wanted to see the sights, I went to a German comedy. Although I did not understand what was being said, I liked the comedy very much, especially when the dancing began. I do not remember ever seeing dancers jump so high. On the next day I saw the emperor ride by. He dresses in French fashion.

The stone tower of St. Stephen's Church is higher than those of Holy Cross in Warsaw.

Contrary to my expectations, Hungarian wine is not as good as that available in our country. I tried to ascertain the reason for this, but the wine merchant who brought samples did not know how to speak Polish, and my cook, who acted as translator, was not at home at the time. I see no statue of King Jan.[65]

Continuing my journey, I departed Vienna December 21, taking the highway to Frankfurt. I stayed there several days, thanks to an attractive and comfortable inn. When I left, the innkeeper demanded that I pay an exorbitant amount because he insisted I had been given a suite of rooms in which the *palatinus rheni*[66] had stayed during the election of the kaiser.

I stayed five whole days in Mainz. Exquisite hams, the finest Rhine wines. I suffered indigestion there, probably from eating ham.

I arrived in Cologne on the Day of Epiphany. I went to the festival at the cathedral and kissed the heads of saints Casper, Melchior, and Balthazar.

Although I rather liked the German lands, I felt as though I had been reborn when I crossed the bridge over the Rhine from the Kiel fortress and found myself in Strasbourg. What a pity that it is winter, for I would have liked to have heard the sound of the birds, who sing more beautifully in France than anywhere else. And the grass here must be greener. As for the cold, though the January day on which I arrived was rather unpleasant, it is considerably less severe than in Poland. I had forgotten to bring a "sleeve" with me,[67] nor had I thought to buy one in Vienna. I ran all over Strasbourg, but there was no white bear cub fur to be had.

Things are really expensive here, as I can gather from the bill the innkeeper presented me. But he is such a polite, such a kind, and also such a handsome fellow that I willingly paid him as much for three days as I paid for a week in Frankfurt. Returning to the matter of the cub fur, it seems most amazing to me that in a city so large, and, moreover, a French city, one cannot obtain what can be gotten so easily in Brody and in Opatów. There must be some secret reason for this, which, God willing, I will get to the bottom of after spending some time in Paris.

The road from Strasbourg is paved and very good, all the way to Paris. In Metz I found a great many Jews. They are attired differently from those in Poland. To my great amazement I recognized there Leiba, the nephew of my Szumin tavern keeper. He told me that he had been sent there for his education by his uncle. The synagogue in Metz is even more beautiful than the one in Brody.

Staying but a short time in Metz, I rode straight through that joyous region where champagne has its origin. In the capital, Rheims, I found to my great dismay that I was unable to view the miraculous ampulla of St. Remi.

Finally, after a rather long, extremely entertaining, and even more expensive trip, on the third of February at 3:00 P.M. I reached Paris.

Chapter Fifteen

The crush of the crowds passing by, the hawkers' cries, the many carriages, the diverse sights, both deafen and delight those who come to Paris for the first time. Such was the state I was in when my carriage entered rue de St. Honoré, one of the most prominent streets in this great city. The building in front of which I alighted was great in size and full of occupants. I was assigned a comfortable suite, where I immediately made myself at home. I say this not without admiration, for what in Warsaw requires so much time to find, namely, good lodging, is available here for foreigners right from the start.

The thought that I was in Paris took possession of me. The satisfaction I felt was inexpressible; I could hardly believe that I was actually in such a desirable place. After a short rest, I asked the innkeeper on what day of the week one could see the ballet and comedy. He replied that because many kinds of entertainment were offered here continuously, I could choose daily between the opera and French or Italian comedy. "Everywhere else," he added, "people think of finding *an* amusement. Here one need only decide which amusement to attend."

I could not control a joyous impulse to grab him by the neck and began to hug the depicter of my happiness heartily. At first he was frightened, but then he smiled, and apparently won over by my candor, he began offering his services to me as one who was a new arrival and lacking in experience. In an instant I found myself surrounded by merchants displaying ever more beautiful goods. A dozen or so tickets and cards were brought to me: some were for a lottery, others lauded select wines, a third set acclaimed new shows, yet others announced a street market. I would never stop talking if I tried to describe in detail all that was to be found on each of them. Hungry for novelty and distracted by ever more pleasing sights, I gazed, read, queried, responded, gave orders— doing all this at once, breathlessly. Hired lackeys and domestics ran back and forth as if competing for my orders. Three-fourths of my rooms were taken up by goods I had purchased. *Two* hired carriages arrived, ordered by messengers who apparently had mixed matters up in all the tumult.

I wanted to go to a comedy. I was sorry I was not going to the opera. The innkeeper praised the Italian theater. Still undecided about where I should go, I paid for and sent back one of the hired carriages. I was about to get into the other, an attractive bright red lacquered one, when I was stopped unexpectedly by the innkeeper: my attire was not entirely appropriate for winter. I asked him to explain why and was told that unsheared velvet is suitable only until *novembre* and that the Belgian lace I had on was not suitable fall wear at all. Reflecting on this and thinking that it would take a lot of time to change my attire, I returned to my lodgings. Having barely tasted the supper brought me, I went to bed, tired by the journey and tired even more from the effort to make myself comfortable. All my attempts to fall asleep, however, were in vain. The constant din of the street and another din of even greater intensity in my head did not permit me to close my eyes.

The following day, while I was being attended in my dressing room by a very fine wigmaker, who was diligently arranging my wig according to the latest fashion, one of the hired lackeys entered and announced Count Fickiewicz. In a moment a beautifully attired young man entered. To my infinite joy and to our mutual amazement, I recognized my beloved neighbor, the subvoivode's son, for whose sister's hand I had had the honor to compete. After the usual initial greetings were exchanged, I asked the count how matters were with him in Paris. "Splendid!" was his response.

He then proceeded to give me a lengthy description of Parisian pastimes and of the civility of Parisian gentlemen, whom he imitated faithfully—even going so far as to have a dress coat designed in the latest French style. On the basis of the various tales he told me, we devised a plan for Paris life. He promised to be my faithful comrade and, in token of our sincere friendship, borrowed 250 louis d'or from me. When I showed him the letters of recommendation from the French envoy in Warsaw, he reproved me, saying that letters addressed to persons whose conversation would be excessively serious held absolutely no promise for vivacious gentlemen as young and fashionable as we. "For you, sir," he continued, "I will find incomparably finer amusements in those houses that I myself frequent."

We then decided, for the honor of Poland, to try to surpass in any and all ways the Parisian gallants in both taste and magnificence.

Thus, the clothing I had brought from Warsaw was at once demeaned. The Drzewica haberdashers' products were not deemed suitable for the festive livery of my servants here. As for myself, I had to wait nearly a week while a carriage, clothing, and livery for four lackeys—two footmen, a Negro, and a hussar—were readied. Only when everything was finally prepared did I set out, under the direction of the count (declaring myself also a count), to enter the haut monde.

The very first visit we paid was to a then-famous dancer of the French opera. I could hardly believe what I saw with my own eyes: the elegant furnishings, the precious jewelry, the vastness of the house, the exquisite table to which I soon had the honor of being admitted. The count informed me that it was necessary to repay such a distinction and taught me how to uphold the glory of Poland by means of costly gifts. I followed his precepts, and armed with a letter of credit and bank drafts in hand, I made frequent visits to my banker. I was amazed by the kindness of the merchants and tradesmen. Everything was given on credit.

My lavish extravagance made me celebrated all over Paris, and my heart was captivated by the charms of one Mademoiselle La Rose.

At her behest I rented a cottage with a beautiful garden in a suburb. And since a French marshal maintained a similar cottage nearby, I furnished mine so nicely that I won over a heretofore unconquerable neighbor.

It was then the fashion in Paris to drive about in light carriages called cabriolets. I ordered four of gold and silver—one for use during each of the four seasons of the year. However, when the time came to venture forth, not being a skilled driver, I turned myself over and onto the cobblestones in the middle of a street, knocking out two teeth, cutting my lip, and dislocating my right leg in the process.

Some kindly people carried me to a nearby barber. Although given excellent care, the verdict I received was distressing: recuperation would take several weeks. The loss of valuable time grieved me. I placed all my hope in the companionship of the count and a dozen or so friends close to my heart.

Chapter Sixteen

I was beginning to feel my old self again, when one day, impatient for the count to come to supper, I sent someone to his lodgings to fetch him. A valet, panting from the errand, reported that the nobleman who was to dine with me was being conducted to a public jail surrounded by city *gensdarmes.*

This perturbed me greatly. Then all of a sudden, a person not known to me delivered the following note:

> Dearest Friend! I beseech you by all that is holy, save me from the depths of despair. I will repay your kindness with my own life if needed.

> Fickiewicz

When I asked the bearer of the note where it had come from, he replied that the count was sitting in the Fort-l'Evêque prison[68] at the insistence of merchants, tradesmen, and other gentlemen to whom he owed significant sums. I wrote the count back immediately, urgently requesting that an account of his debts be sent. In an hour the account was brought. The debts totaled 2,719 Polish zloty. Magnanimity and national honor superseded economic considerations. I vouched for the count on the basis of my good financial standing, and an order freeing him was immediately issued.

To celebrate this heroic action, I invited all our common friends to supper, sending my fancy carriage for the count. He was not to be found at the prison or, what is worse, at his lodgings. All the innkeeper could tell my men was that His Honor the count, having quickly exchanged what remained of his household effects for cash, had boarded a post chaise and left Paris.

That good is paid back with evil is what sad experience has taught me. Had this brought an end to my foolish behavior, the matter would have been quite bearable. However, after a year's sojourn in Paris, during which the drafts sent from Poland on three occasions paid only half of what I owed, my banker did not want to extend me further credit. The merchants and tradesmen began to make a nuisance of themselves. Wishing to appease those to whom I owed debts, I wrote home for the necessary money.

Impatiently awaiting a reply with the remittance, I received instead a letter informing me that my old adversary had won the lawsuit after all. He had forced my plenipotentiary to yield his authority and had seized the unencumbered part of my estate—Szumin and its environs—for the property damage I had acknowledged, legal expenses, expulsion fines, and other money due him.

The fancy clothes and other valuables I repeatedly pawned to moneylenders continued to provide me some credit and a modicum of elegance. These too ran out, and creditors to whom I had given guarantees on the count's behalf began court action. Having no means to assuage them and fearing that I would suffer my friend's fate, I cashed in my remaining valuables on the sly and under the pretext of taking a drive mounted the first post horse I could lay hands on. Pretending to be a courier, I decamped with such alacrity that I was at the border of Austrian Flanders the next day.[69] Spending only a night in Mons, I set out for Holland and, without stopping anywhere, reached Amsterdam.

At another time this trading capital of the entire world, which held the prospect of innumerable sights of interest, might have provided me with endless entertainment. In my present circumstances, I could think of nothing but myself. Stripped of my possessions, weighed down by debt at home and abroad, I considered myself a ruined man. Desperate thoughts made it impossible for me to concentrate.

One day, plagued by such thoughts while walking near the port, I was approached by a captain of a ship about to set sail. When he asked me the cause of my profound melancholy, I bared my soul to him. Upon learning that he was sailing to Batavia, I immediately thought that I too should set out for that land. He willingly accepted my request to accompany him, and on the very next day, when favorable winds came up, we set sail.

Chapter Seventeen

We were on a man-of-war armed with sixty cannon that was transporting government officials to Batavia. Besides sailors and soldiers, there were a dozen or so travelers. The first pitching of the boat caused me to suffer greatly, a customary reaction in such circumstances. Little by little I adapted to the existence of being on board ship. Consistently favorable winds drove us in a reasonably short time to the Canary Islands. There we went ashore for fresh water and provisions. Several times adverse winds forced us to disembark on the shores of Africa for respite.

The lands I saw are well known thanks to the accounts of various travelers. I do not believe that it is necessary to repeat what others have already said. When we reached the Cape of Good Hope, where Africa ends, a heavy snow violently battered our ship. And since a period of unfavorable weather set in, preventing us from sailing on, we spent several months here. The trip to Batavia was canceled, and worse still, the commanding officer, who had occupied an important post under the Republic, had to return home.[70]

His successor was a severe and ill-mannered man, like many such people who spend their lives at sea. I would have been content to remain in that place but saw no way to earn a living. Thus, following the former commander's advice and aided by his letters of introduction, I set sail for Batavia. Thanks to fairly good winds, we had completed a significant part of the trip when all the winds grew calm and the ship came to a halt in the middle of the ocean. The sea, like a mirror, displayed not the slightest movement, and extreme heat tormented us greatly. The provisions began to spoil, and we were running out of drinking water. By the twelfth day of this unbearable stillness, we reckoned that half of the people on board were sick.

Suddenly the wind came up, but it was so strong a wind that we had to lower most of the sails. The anchors were lowered several times, but they could not hold us. The entire crew was gripped by the terrible fear that so much wind, blowing us in a completely opposite direction from the one in which we were headed, would take us to an unknown land. The storm continued unabated for six days. The winds intensified, the mainmast broke. Most people on board were incapable of working because of discomfort, sickness, and exhaustion. Fortifying myself as best I could, I pumped out water left by the immense waves that were inundating our ship. Suddenly one of the sailors shouted that land was nigh. His cry, though desirable in other circumstances, seemed to all of us like a death knell. In an instant the ship, driven onto rocks, was shattered by a terrible crash.

What happened to me then, I cannot say. I do know that, coming to, I found myself surrounded by the ocean. Battered by the waves and swollen with seawater, I began to gather what strength I had left. By luck I caught hold of a fairly large plank. I gripped it and held it so tightly that, despite the constant tossing and rising and falling of the waves, I was thrown half alive onto the sandy shore. Afraid that the undertow would sweep me back, I ran breathlessly over the sand. My strength deserted me, and I fell unconscious.

End of Book One

BOOK TWO

Chapter One

At first there was nausea; after that sleep came and cut short my misery. I slept for a long time and only opened my eyes when the sun with all its brilliance began to strike them. Once awake, I regretted that I had not shut my eyes for the last time. My strength, which had been drained out of me, was beginning to return, but when I reflected on my situation, the only thing that eased my despair was the thought of death. I certainly would have taken my life had not religious feelings instilled in my youth stayed the hands ready to carry out this act. Horrified by the extreme to which I had been driven by vile despair, I lifted my eyes to heaven. At once a ray of fresh hope stole its way into my heart. I raised my hands and began to cry for help to that Providential Being who commands all of creation and who stubbornly refuses to abandon even its most despicable creature.

I got up and, as there was no help or hope now possible from the sea, set out for the interior of that land to which the unforeseen vicissitudes of fate had brought me. I feared that I would be attacked by predatory beasts. The sight of new and curious objects, however, amused and amazed me, for almost all the trees, fruit, and herbage were different from those of Europe. I had gone nearly a half mile through very dense forest without seeing a trace of the smallest road or path when to my joy I noticed that the trees were beginning to thin out. At last I emerged into a field, and noticing that it had been assiduously cultivated and was covered with grain that was nearly ripe, I rejoiced still more, concluding that this land not only was inhabited but was inhabited by people who were not savages, since they were acquainted with agriculture and constituted a community. This opinion was soon confirmed by the welcome sight of a hamlet or village. While the houses did not seem either luxurious or lofty, they were ample and constructed with a symmetry pleasing to the eye.

I approached the place eagerly and saw a fairly large crowd of people watching some sort of pageant. From afar they soon noticed my dress, which apparently was something not seen in those parts. They all moved toward me, and in the twinkling of an eye I was surrounded by people who examined me curiously. Our mutual wonder lasted for several minutes. Then a dignified old man approached me; when he gave me his hand as a sign of welcome, I fell to his feet and shed bitter tears. He raised me up eagerly and began to speak gently, as I was able to surmise from his look and gestures, for the tongue in which he spoke was totally foreign to me.

On the chance that he might understand, I began to speak to him first in Polish, then in Latin, and finally in French. But since he did not comprehend me, I described my present circumstances by means of gestures, depicting as best I could how I had set out by sea from very distant lands, how my ship had been wrecked and my companions drowned, and how I had escaped death by clinging to a plank. I could tell they understood that I had come by sea. But they were unable to comprehend the ship I described and the distant land from which I had come. Because hunger was beginning to gnaw at me, I asked by means of a gesture for a meal. Observing my need, the old man took me by the hand and led me to his own home. Like the others, it was neither lofty nor grand. Cleanliness, order, and symmetry were its finest adornments. The houses were all frame with shiny walls inside and out. The wood must have been coated with a special varnish, because it was impossible to believe that wood could naturally be that way. The first room had benches all around it, raised a little above the floor. It was here that I was seated by my host. The gray-haired woman who came when called appeared to be his wife. At first she was astonished when her husband recounted how I had arrived. She then greeted me by placing her hands over her heart. A little table was set before me, and in no time I was served vegetables, dairy products, and fruit and was given water to drink.

Even though I had appeased the hunger gnawing at me, I was unable to stop eating the vegetables, for I enjoyed their unusual taste and seasoning. The fruit was incomparably better than ours, the bread similar to our rye, only tastier. I was given only a spoon to eat with. Wanting to cut the bread, I got my knife out of my pocket. This tool, probably unknown in this land, greatly amazed my host. He examined it with great curiosity, but it seemed to me that he did not dare touch it. When I offered it to him, he took hold of it by means of the blade and cut one of his fingers. Seeing blood, he threw the knife on the ground, cried out, and, when the other members of the household came running, told them what had happened. I wanted to pick the knife up, but they would not allow me to do so. It was difficult to keep from laughing when a short while later they brought a tool that resembled a rake and gingerly pushed my knife toward the door. Throwing it out, they watched it from a distance as if to assure themselves that it would not move on its own. Then they dug a rather deep hole and buried it in the earth.

After this my host came up to me and, as I understood from his gestures, reproached me for exposing him to such great danger. He asked whether there was another such object in my possession. I responded negatively. He then beseeched me not to touch the buried knife. I promised willingly, and he squeezed my hand as a sign of friendship and led me to his garden, or, rather, to the orchard behind his house. There trees planted in rows were laden with various types of fruit. In place of a fence or hedge, a narrow ditch—designed more, it would seem, for drainage than as a safeguard—separated my host's orchard from that of his neighbor. In the middle of the orchard was a pond, and the stream that passed through it also filled the pond in the neighbor's orchard. Later I learned that orchards were planted adjacent to one another so that all the inhabitants of the settlement might take advantage of this system.

When it had begun to get dark outside, the lamp that hung in the middle of the room was lighted, and we sat down to supper. In addition to the host and his wife, there were three grown sons and, it seemed, two grandchildren. When the meal ended, everyone rose and faced east, and the host, lifting his eyes toward heaven, in a clear voice uttered a prayer of thanksgiving. After he had embraced the children one by one, he took me by the hand and led me to a separate room. There I found a pallet that served as a mattress, a pillow, and a large counterpane, all made out of materials unknown to me.

Chapter Two

When I awoke, I resolved then and there to learn the language of this land. For without knowing the language, I knew it would be virtually impossible for me to familiarize myself with local laws and customs, to understand the inhabitants' way of thinking, and to return the debt of gratitude I owed them for receiving me so kindly. For the present I paid close attention to whatever came to my attention.

The settlement in which I was staying had 120 households, each with a home, field, and garden; all were equal in size. More often than not the children worked for their parents. The household included servants as well, both male and female, but no distinctions whatsoever were drawn in either dress or amenities between them and other members of the household. Consequently, there was not the slightest trace of obsequiousness among these serving people. Masters did not look upon them with a severe eye, nor did I ever see any evidence of painful or abusive punishment. The inhabitants were of average height, their faces cheerful, their complexions healthy. I saw neither cripples nor excessively obese or terribly thin people. Gray hair, not decrepitude, marked the elderly.

Powder might have helped the women, had not a thousand charms more than compensated for their somewhat swarthy complexions. On the other hand, no red pigment could match the beauty and vigor of their ruddy cheeks, which any embarrassment set afire. It seemed to me that the painted faces I had left behind were very mediocre copies and that I was now observing choice originals.

The men's attire was fashioned from a very simple kind of

material, and yet it was so generously cut that it did not restrict the limbs the way our clothing does. All the clothing was grayish or white in hue, depending on the wool used, for it was left undyed. I saw very few black sheep; what is more, wool of that color was used for counterpanes and mattresses. The style of clothing was similar to what we associate with Greek and Roman statues. There was an undergarment that draped to a point below the knees and an outer one, far longer and more ample, that resembled a cloak and was worn primarily by the older people, though also by younger people in times of cold or rainy weather. The men wore their hair neck-length, combed back to keep it out of the eyes. The children's hair was cut short for the sake of neatness.

The women's clothing was made of a more delicate material and was styled somewhat differently. The fashion of applying white or grayish powder had not yet invaded this land, and the local ladies would have considered it untidy to grease the hair with pomade. That is not to say, however, that women here did not wear handsome or even elegant dress. The desire to be attractive is everywhere characteristic of the fair sex.

Changes in fashion were unknown. Clothing styles had been the same for eons. Colors never changed, since the local inhabitants did not know the secret of dying wool. I learned subsequently that when my clothes were examined (these included a green cloak and a crimson vest), they immediately concluded that the sheep in my country were green and crimson.

The land was washed on all sides by the sea, and the island was known as Nipu. The language used by the people was fairly easy, but limited. In order to make them understand the many luxuries we enjoy and how they were made, I had to provide detailed explanations and draw analogies. The Nipuans had no words for falsehood, theft, treason, or flattery. They were unaware of legal terminology. They did not have special names for different ailments. Nor did they have courtiers, lawyers, or doctors.

Guided by my host, I spent time learning the Nipuan language. Indeed, within a few months I could begin to make myself understood. During this whole time I noticed that the Nipuans avoided me. When it was absolutely necessary for them to deal with me, they showed me every kindness. My questions were answered, but the superficial responses given indicated a certain constraint and antipathy. The Nipuans' lack of trust and extreme caution distressed me, but I decided that there must be reasons for this, which, though unknown to me, were to their way of thinking honest and proper. Even my host, when questioned by me about the customs, laws, and history of the land, avoided giving direct answers. Afraid of appearing indiscreet, I tended to lapse into silence. On the other hand, because my host was most interested in learning even the smallest details about European countries, I tried as best I could to satisfy his curiosity and oblige him.

One day, when I was strolling along absorbed in thoughts such as these, my host came up to me with a cheerful face and announced that on the next day I would be accepted into the community.

Chapter Three

I was anxious to find out what rites of acceptance would accompany my being admitted into Nipuan society. Knowing that the Nipuans were obliging and decent, yet uncivilized and unenlightened with regard to learning, the arts, and the way in which they conducted their lives, I decided that I could best show my gratitude by making them aware of their lack of knowledge and their naïveté. With this in mind, I composed a speech, which I intended to deliver the next day, exhorting them to give up their uncivilized ways and follow in the footsteps of Europeans, who surpass all other peoples in accomplishments and knowledge.

Noon was already approaching when my host came to conduct me to the house in the settlement where all the householders had gathered. I was received warmly, and we sat down at earthen tables in the cool shade of the orchard where the usual dishes were set before us. As the meal was drawing to a close, the eldest of those at the table summoned me and said: "My Brother! Stay with us, take advantage of nature's gifts; remember that we are obliged to live in love and harmony."

He then broke off a chunk of bread and, dividing it into two pieces, put one piece into his mouth and handed me the other. I accepted it respectfully and consumed it and was about to enlighten these good but uncivilized people when my host began to speak as follows: "This man, whom you charged me to instruct, has conducted himself commendably in my household. He has already completed the first steps. While his way of thinking, speaking, and behaving are wrong, one must take pity on the ignorance, naïveté, and blindness of one who certainly should not be blamed for having been born among crude and uncivilized people. At present Xaoo does not have a helper. He can take in this man and both teach and employ him…"

I completely forgot my oration, so taken aback was I by these unexpected words. I who wished to teach these simple and un-civilized beings reason was judged by *them* to be uncivilized and in need of enlightenment. I sat with downcast eyes, sunk in thought, when this Xaoo, I knew not whether master or teacher, took me by the hand and led me to his home. After showing me about the barnyard, the cow shed, the barn, and the field, he divided the day's work into two parts: in the morning I was to go out into the field to work; the remainder of the time I was to spend looking after things that needed to be done in and around the household.

I never would have thought that someday I would become a plowman. It was important, however, to make a virtue out of necessity and to make a courageous start on what was really a new type of apprenticeship rather than schooling. Had my own master and teacher not presented himself as an example, my situation would have seemed unbearable. My labors were ennobled by his company and our common effort. Little by little I rid myself of my aversion to "menial" work. In time I grew to recognize the injustice of that prejudice that deems husbandry and all other aspects of the farmer's trade shameful.

I waited impatiently for at least some semblance of the education I expected to receive. But nothing my teacher's lips emitted could be construed as such. When we walked together to work, he plied me incessantly with questions, just as my first host had done, making it apparent that he wished to be as fully informed as possible not only about European customs, laws, writing, and arts but also about my way of thinking.

Chapter Four

About three months into my stay, as Xaoo was taking me into the field with him, he changed the way he spoke to me. Now, instead of asking questions, he began to persuade me that everyone needs to be able to suppress his evil inclinations and to eradicate prejudice. His words were simple and few, yet to the point. Moreover, they were ordered in such a way that one subject led readily to another, the entire discourse being like a complex and cohesive logical chain made up of absolutely indispensable links. He compared education to agriculture.

"One must first get to know the land," he said, "in order to know how to set about cultivating it, especially when tilling new soil. If one clears land for a field where there have been bushes and trees, one should not merely cut down the trees and saw off the bushes; one must try as hard as one can to dig out of the ground the roots of the trees and shrubs. If one does not do this, the roots will occupy much of the land, and the plow will strike them and break. Moreover, if the roots remain in the soil, they will continually produce harmful and worthless shoots. If there are no trees or bushes in the new soil, weeds will spring up, which, though weak of root, will grow even more thickly. A good tiller of the soil thus will not begrudge the task of pulling out the little bunches of roots one by one. What is more, one will be able to profit from the roots, using their ashes to enrich the virgin land. On the other hand, it is frivolous and unreasonable to root out the passions in man. As the elements sustain the body, so the passions sustain the mind. Like roots, they cause wrongdoing only if used improperly.

"From the answers you have given to my questions I have come to know that in your part of the world, at least so it seems to me, either intellectual conviction or some sort of salutary and fortunate instinct has caused men, or, better still, impelled them, to educate their young. Despite all this I dare contend that you are gravely mistaken about both the manner and the particular stages of education. What would you say about a builder who wanted to start a house with the roof or who made the floor without having put up walls? You would laugh at the carpenter's stupidity, for it would seem unlikely to you that such a house could be built. You should understand that the house is you, and the one who taught you is the carpenter.

"Your tainted intellect has concocted some sort of curious studies that we by the grace of the Supreme Being do not have or wish to have here.

"You told me that as an infant, not long after you began to talk, you were instructed to call everything by a different name from that you had hitherto used. And when you had learned this other, new name, you had to learn to call things by yet other names. If this is not the height of insanity, please tell me. If this practice of forever renaming things gained you better knowledge of them, I would judge it to be no more than a bad idea for all the difficulties caused. And seeing a good result, I would forgive you the wrong means. But if, as you yourself say, the only advantage to this is that you can speak with some people so that others present do not understand, I utterly fail to see any gain or good in it, for it produces only anger and folly. Anger, for to speak so that another does not understand is to annoy that other person, to make him suspicious and distrustful, to create an aura of superiority or refinement that the one who does not understand will find demeaning. Folly, for one's labor results in absolutely no gain.

"You mentioned books, writing, and symbols that, if one knows many languages, can be read and comprehended and thereby may help one achieve ever-greater excellence. If we grant that one cannot learn except by means of symbols representing the sounds of words, why do you not employ these symbols as a single system for naming things?

"Taught in this manner from early childhood, the pupil, rather than gaining the correct knowledge of an object or idea, will find his memory cluttered with names. Terrified at the very outset by the difficulty of learning in this way, if by nature he does not grasp things readily, he will acquire such knowledge only through dint of great effort. If he has a mind for it, he will, to be sure, learn the names but in doing so will sustain damage twice over: he will lose time that might be spent on more necessary things, and he will develop a distaste for other knowledge more appropriate to someone in his position.

"You have two ways of revealing your thoughts: by the normal mode of discourse or by arranging words in such a way as to produce a special sound pattern characterized by musical harmony. Both these ways are known to us—and please do not think that we despise that which you call rhetoric and poetry.

"The gift of speech is too important a matter to be overlooked in the education of the young. We know that words properly arranged proclaim thought more effectively and frequently captivate people's minds by virtue of their gentle strength. You have heard the melodiousness and experienced the grace of the rhymed verses in the songs of Nipu. These songs express our gratitude to the Supreme Being and extol the virtues of our ancestors in order to encourage descendants to emulate them. Doubtless we would have attached less importance to poetry had we not recognized that rhythmic structures better inculcate in the mind and memory things that we wish our young people to learn and to remember.

"In your country, as you have told me, there are people who hold eloquence in contempt and do not wish the young to be trained in it. They do ill. I do not perceive the source of their error. And though I do not thoroughly understand your way of thinking, I would hazard a guess that such people act this way either because they judge the art of speaking well to be a characteristic of great intellects alone, or because they envy those who have a command of something they lack, or because they are greatly concerned lest eloquence be misused. If the last truly posed a threat, then virtue would have to be abandoned lest hypocrisy reign supreme. If such people fear that the young will grow accustomed to loquaciousness rather than to eloquence, they themselves should serve as an example and not go to extremes in their search for sophisticated words, complex expressions, and an extraordinary style. If they must condemn eloquence, then let them do so in simple and ordinary language.

"Wishing to provide an example of your oratory, you repeated to me the speech you had prepared to deliver during the communal feast. I remember several of your expressions. They had a rather smooth sound. You used several hundred words, however, to express something you might have stated in a dozen, or certainly in no more than twenty words. It is good that you did not give that speech. For by wrapping up its contents in so many unnecessary words, you ran the risk of being judged a frivolous person who merely likes to play with the arrangement of words, or a foolish person who does not know how to express himself, or a cunning person who wants to suppress the truth, or a proud person who seeks praise and nothing more. I do not ponder the aim of your speech. You yourself sensed that it is neither proper nor appropriate for a person who knows neither himself nor others to deem others savages and himself a teacher."

Chapter Five

My teacher's speech altered the way I thought about that which we consider savagery. To acknowledge that I myself was a savage would have meant humbling myself too much and behaving in a way contrary to my own convictions. After all that I had seen and heard, however, I could not judge the inhabitants of this land to be uncivilized. Xaoo's reasoning humbled me. I could not fathom how a person who had not been to Warsaw and had not seen Paris was able nonetheless to think and speak sensibly and to be convincing, even in conversation with someone who had both seen and heard incomparably more than he. I was sunk in thoughts such as these when Xaoo came to fetch me. As we went to work in the field he continued the speech begun the day before:

"Yesterday we spoke about eloquence, the study of languages, and poetry. This is all founded on a knowledge of words and how they are arranged. Let us get to the heart of the matter. When I asked you whether anything else is taught in your land, I was really overwhelmed by the many pompous titles of the various subjects you enumerated. Since you named history first, I assume that it is considered more important than the others.

"Knowledge of the history of one's own country is an extremely useful thing. For recounting the praiseworthy deeds of one's forefathers inspires emulation among the descendants and instills greater respect for and love of one's native land. It acts, as it were, as a school of good morals. This, at least, is the way we regard and define the history of our land. As you know, we do not have books, and we do not have an alphabet. Nonetheless, truthful tales, passed down from one generation to the next, depict in a lively yet detailed manner all that has happened in our land. The oldest member of the family knows enough about his forebears from ancient times so that each time he gives instruction to his own children, he can build upon examples drawn from these forebears' way of life. The dignity of the teller, the noble heritage, the way in which the narration is delivered, and the youthfulness of the listeners combine to make a lasting impression.

"You have told me that in your country history is incomparably broader. There are as many kinds of history, you said, as there are ways of speaking. From this I must conclude that the history of your native land either is very unimportant or is not given precedence over the history of other lands. While it is good to know what has happened to other people in order to profit from the examples foreigners can provide, the first goal of every citizen's education must be knowledge of his own country's history.

"As for history in general, if you choose to found it on facts— what year and day something may have happened—if you call it a science that deals with the surnames of people who came before you, or if you make a record of general events without discussing individuals, it will do nothing more than clutter the memory. Study of such history is futile. If you attempt to find out what has happened at a neighbor's without first knowing or caring to find out what has happened in your own house, you are not a worthy member of society.

"You have given me grounds to think that the society into which you were born cares for neither its own country nor its language. To draw a general comparison, that which we have in our own possession may in this or that respect be less ideal than that which others possess. But here self-love, or what we call love of country, comes to the rescue. It weakens our vices and hides our shortcomings to as great a degree as possible. Self-love can be prudent; it can help us improve our well-being by taking legitimate advantage of our neighbor's kindliness.

"Disdain for one's own country and language denotes a frivolous mind and a false heart. In your country you are guilty of this and therefore of having a vile and harmful impact. You abandon your own language, and you order your children to study foreign ones as diligently as possible. You disregard information about events in your own country and compel your young people to know without fail what has happened abroad. Do you know what the consequences of this are? A child observes that his native language does not require study but that foreign ones demand it and decides that the latter are superior. Preoccupied with foreign events, dazzled by descriptions—some of them probably fanciful—of other countries, he despises what he sees constantly before him and longs to see that which only seems more beautiful in his overwrought imagination.

"Descriptions of countries you call geography. The reason we are curious about neighbors' activities is the same reason you compose geographical descriptions of the location and distinguishing characteristics of countries, the form of government of each nation, and other such facts. Since we are not in contact with other societies, we have no need for this science. And although we might be enlightened to some degree by it, for various reasons I would prefer that we remain ignorant."

Chapter Six

I listened to my teacher's speeches with considerable relish. Normally they were preceded by questions. Before beginning to speak about education, the arts, or other subjects relating to Europe, he would first repeat the definitions or descriptions of them that I had furnished earlier. He would then ask additional questions, trying to obtain even fuller explanations of matters about which he intended to speak with me. Only when he thought that he had enough information did he treat a subject in detail, patiently listening to my objections. And if I did not react, he would prompt me to reveal any doubts I had and to question any judgments of his that did not agree with my way of thinking. He was incapable of projecting an image of sublime melancholy. He was incapable of being forever absorbed in thought or of giving the appearance of such. Absent-mindedness, which adorns and distinguishes our sages to so great a degree, was alien to him. The tone of his voice was not lofty. He did not try to define anything he did not know. Yet he was not an uncivilized being.

When I described philosophy to him as best I could and explained that part of it that deals with manners and mores, he exclaimed joyfully: "That's precisely what our education is, and that is the school you are now attending. I wish to fix its maxims, its simple rules, not in your memory but in your heart. In your land this subject may depend on words. We are less concerned with definitions; we would rather have people fulfill their responsibilities.

"Philosophy, which you told me means 'love of wisdom,' ought to have as its chief aim knowledge of man's responsibilities and the fulfillment of those responsibilities. In your opinion this subject is a very difficult one and strains one's intellect more than any other. I'm not surprised to hear this when I learn what you include under this general term. With metaphysics you plunge into the realm of intangibles. Any subject that exceeds the natural comprehension of things must indeed be extremely difficult.

"Physics deals with the nature of things, but you venture too far with it also. Your excessively proud intellect desires to raise a veil lowered before the dawn of time. You wish to persuade those less knowledgeable that you have raised it, but instead of giving the substance of things revealed, you report your dreams and delusions.[71] You fly about the heavens. Not content with the pleasing sight of stars and planets, you want to measure them. Your impudent curiosity exceeds normal bounds, often neglecting that which is within your range of vision and could be investigated and understood with serious effort. And since all the decrees of nature are uncanny, you should know that whatever the Supreme Being permits you to understand can be used to benefit you.

"You see that the ground is covered with herbage. It has not shot up solely in order to please the eye. Concealed in this herbage is a mystery beneficial to you. To investigate this mystery, to test and know it, is an appropriate, absorbing, and at the same time useful occupation. The firmament of stars twinkles. Because of vain haughtiness, it has been made a prophetic book, and the desire has emerged to read the hidden future in its regular movements.

"Nature, which does nothing without a purpose, in bestowing upon the intellect the desire to investigate, wished prudence to be its guide. Nature wanted our curiosity to be focused solely on those things that can be readily investigated and, having been investigated, be of use. Whatever else we strive to do is then nothing more than a demonstration of our haughtiness and imperfection.

"That which you call logic is characteristic of an intellect that is not burdened by trifles and prejudices. But take care that your imagination does not attempt to soar to heights too great. Permit your mind to pursue soberly a single goal and nothing more. Even if the rules of formal reasoning are not followed, your thinking will then proceed along proper lines.

"After all that has been said about education and about subjects of study in your land, the following observations can be made: First of all, your education, in terms of both objectives and methods, is perverse. Second, you impede its progress by becoming encumbered with petty matters. Third, you are overconfident about your powers of reasoning. All kinds of prejudice cloud your intellect. Fourth, fickleness and thoughtlessness guide and take control of you. Lastly, an entirely unjustifiable ambition has blinded all of you to such a degree that you have an extremely high opinion of yourselves. Therefore, you take for granted, on the one hand, that your inner excellence is lacking in nothing and, on the other, that to satisfy your outer happiness you are in need of everything.

"Having judged yourselves to be the most accomplished people ever, you wish to have bestowed on you what you consider your just deserts, the choicest gifts of nature. From this it follows that your land is beneath the likes of you. Its language is too lowly to embrace and convey your lofty thoughts; and to associate there with those of nonnoble birth is unseemly. In short, the greater value you place on yourselves, the unhappier you become. If what you represent is perfection and refinement, and if what we represent is the uncivilized, simple, and coarse, then it seems to me that it is better to be like us, uncivilized."

Chapter Seven

Above I mentioned that, having been judged uncivilized, I had been consigned to a farmer for instruction. For a fairly long time I performed all the tasks of a plowman rather than those of a pupil. In this school I learned firsthand how to sow, mow, and reap rather than studying rules about how one ought to sow, mow, and reap. Seeing the farm folk, I asked my master once in the midst of work whether they, like our farmers, did not rely on agronomical speculation, using an ephemeris of their own. He stared at me in wonder, shook his head, and kept mowing, paying my question no heed.

About midday, as we ate in the shade of the trees, he asked me what I understood the word *agronomy* to mean. I replied that it is an extremely useful science thanks to which the art of farming is perfected and natural wealth is multiplied. This science thus embraces everything that makes for the happiness of a country, particularly of its inhabitants.[72] "What a pity," I said further, "that this treasure has remained buried until now. Undoubtedly there would otherwise have been much less unhappiness in the world and many fewer revolutions recounted in our histories."

"Who was it that perfected the art of farming?" asked Xaoo. "Undoubtedly a diligent farmer taught by long experience who somehow understood certain secrets unknown to his fellow farmers."

"You are wrong," said I. "These things are described in books, and our farmers do not know how to write. Those who revealed the secrets to us for the most part probably never saw soil being tilled. But they are worthy of great admiration because by dint of their intellect they discovered something that their ancestors with their continual toiling on the land could not."

My speech was cut short by his laughter. This lack of respect for the clever inventions of our age made me angry. I thought to myself, however, that I should have sympathy for Xaoo's simple nature. I did not want to shame and humiliate him with my irrefutable arguments. And so we proceeded to bind sheaves, something he, a simple old man, though ignorant of agronomy, nevertheless did better and faster than I.

The Nipuans taught me by their example that excellent farming does not demand eloquent speculation. Their unsophisticated observations were based solely on experience. Moreover, their methods were all easy to understand, cheap, and not difficult to follow. Their fine methods of farming were justified by the results: there was not so much as a mention of hunger on Nipu. And if a year turned out to be unproductive, no one felt want because of all the reserves from the previous years' harvests.

I myself experienced the beneficial effects of farming. The work, which at first seemed unbearable to me, became in time a pleasant occupation. The convulsions, miasmas, and rheumatisms from which the waters of Selters and Karlsbad were unable to extricate me receded on their own with the heavy sweat. The appetite that earlier my German cook, Christian, and later M. Sosancourt, a Frenchman, had to rouse and brace with rich broths, returned by itself; the turnip eaten after work tasted better than the partridge I had once had in my native Podlasie.

Work and uncluttered thoughts invigorated my once-weakened temperament. For want of a looking glass I gazed at my reflection in the water and saw that my complexion to be sure had become swarthy, but that my face was full and had a rosy vitality to it. Sound, uninterrupted sleep put vigor into limbs exhausted by daily labor. And the work made me more robust every day.

Chapter Eight

Once while walking in the orchard with my teacher I noticed the hole where my knife was buried and was unable to refrain from smiling. Xaoo was quick to notice this and immediately reacted: "Your amusement is justified, and it does not really offend me because I saw that you wanted to conceal it. To mock someone else's ignorance is cruel, but to completely subdue an instantaneous reaction is difficult. When your knife hurt my neighbor, our ignorance of the nature of metals, the unusual shape of this implement, the gleam of its shiny blade, and the way it injured the neighbor's finger produced in us an initial response of terror—terror great enough to make us decide that your knife was a living and destructive being.

"Your arrival by sea from another world led us to believe the most incredible things. And although ignorant, we eventually did the right thing. If I had known then what I know now about what you use iron for, I would truly have idolized you for returning that destructive metal to the earth. You, who in your blasphemous impudence complain that Providence has given you too short a time in which to live, search for clever ways to cut life short. And as if that were not enough, thanks to your immoderate ways, you shorten your own days, inventing ever more powerful ways of destroying yourselves."

In order to salvage my compatriots' reputation somewhat, I had deliberately concealed from Xaoo the fact that we practice the art of war. He discovered my dishonesty and consequently urged me to give him detailed information on this subject. In an effort to lessen as best I could the poor opinion he had of us already, I began by explaining to him about the multitude of peoples on the earth and how nations differ not only in dress and speech but also in customs and in their likes and dislikes. Because of these differences it was only natural that discord should arise and, hence, the need for arms to defend oneself from the incursions of neighbors, to protect the weak against those more powerful, and to curb unjustifiable acts of violence.

Metal ore, extracted by accident from the earth, was employed for a long time in agriculture and in construction, I observed. It was used to make things that man because of his industriousness found necessary to invent. And since even the best things are corrupted when used by the wrong people, iron in the hands of the unrighteous was turned into a harmful tool, an instrument for the destruction of human life. Armed skirmishes between individual persons, societies, and nations were the result.

As time went on, it became harder and harder to avert evil because evil had become deeply rooted and was everywhere. Hence upright and enlightened men in written and spoken word and lawmakers through legislation justified wars under certain circumstances and promulgated rules for practicing this nefarious art in order to limit its fatal consequences. The commander leading the army that defended the fatherland became a highly esteemed citizen, a soldier dying on a battlefield a sacrifice for the common good. Little by little, however, aversion to this inherently brutal craft disappeared, and what we as true human beings had once called force, savagery, and ferocity was renamed courage, prowess, and heroism by the general public.

"What you told me earlier about your jurists being most eloquent when they are defending wicked causes no longer surprises me," said Xaoo. "You yourself are evidence of this, though doubtless that wasn't your intent. You may excuse the art of war as much as you like, but your society deserves to be pitied rather than praised for it.

"In a large group of people differences in character can cause squabbles. That this could lead eventually to loss of life is, however, something we do not know. You must possess intense emotions, more intense than we, to have this happen. You enumerated in a facetious and witty manner those unfortunate discoveries that have led to the manufacture of weapons out of metal. Upright men, you say, wrote and spoke out against such wickedness, lawmakers wished to eradicate it, but their exertions and efforts were in vain. These upright men must indeed have been quite unusual by the standards of your society if they could not find enough like-minded people to join them in writing, speaking out, and demonstrating against this evil in the early stages of its development.

"I am particularly surprised that lawmakers were unable to prevent this from happening. May I ask why you erect vain statues to such people if the power you have given them is meaningless because of your own obstinacy? Why do you write laws if you have no intention of obeying them? I may be mistaken, but it seems to me that the writings of your upright citizens and the acts your lawmakers passed must have been insincere and superficial. Disenchanted by the results of their first efforts, they abandoned the original strictness of their tracts and laws and, instead of trying to extirpate this vice, chose to make it seem less harmful. In this way they justified crime to their people. Men of real courage do not lose heart if things do not begin well. Moreover, persistent and firm opposition will sooner or later vanquish even the most deeply rooted fault.

"I am not, nor could I be, an admirer of a situation in which one person or a small group of people govern the rest. But in such instances I am thoroughly convinced that anyone who wants to govern his fellow men must arm himself with dauntless courage. If the smallest chink in this armor is visible to those governed, the faith they have in their own might will increase twofold. They will cast off the yoke of what you call beneficial subordination, and one of the very well educated may then dispel any illusions the public has, illusions, I daresay, greatly to the advantage of the one who commands.

"I understand that the discovery of metals was a most useful discovery for various crafts. But you have paid too dearly for the benefits it produced. Luxury leads to greater needs than those prescribed by nature, where needs are satisfied without the help of gold, silver, iron, and copper. While it is true that tools made of metal save time and effort, a combination of ingenuity and patience can compensate for this, as you have witnessed here. I admit that this necessarily entails more work, but work is in itself so beneficial that to spare oneself work is to commit a grave injustice against oneself. Nature has taught us what it is that we truly need. And she has also given us the instinct to satisfy that need."

Chapter Nine

Once Xaoo took me with him when he had to go on a fairly long trip. This was the first time I had a chance to see more of this rather large land. When I asked how big Nipu was, Xaoo replied that it took eleven days to walk directly from one coast to the other and that the island was nearly as wide as it was long. Wherever we went we saw well-cultivated fields. Homesteads were fairly numerous, and each had a woodlot large enough to supply its needs. From the even way in which the land was divided, I could tell that when there was more than enough land for plots, the leftover area was turned into fields. In places where land was scarce, individual plots were sown with great care.

On the eighth day of our trip, Xaoo pointed to a field on the left that was quite large and surrounded by beautiful trees. In the middle of the field was a small building decorated more elaborately than most. When we approached it, a dignified old man emerged from a house nearby. He greeted us hospitably and conducted us to the door. When Xaoo reached the building, he stopped and said: "I greet you, sweet memory of our father!"

Inside was an extraordinarily clean and tidy chamber, in the middle of which stood a very well-made cabinet. The old man opened the cabinet. I expected to see something special in it, but to my great surprise I saw only a set of farming implements so old that they were nearly falling apart. The two old men took them reverently into their hands. Xaoo, knowing how curious I must be, said: "The field that surrounds this building was cleared and cultivated by the hands of the father of us all. Kootes himself used these implements, and we have preserved them from time immemorial. Kootes, perhaps in the same way as you, came from a foreign land with his wife and two children to what was then an uninhabited island and with his own hands cleared the land. The Supreme Being looked favorably upon his labor: he lived long enough to see the fourth generation of his family born. His precepts still seem fresh in our memory. The farming implements he used are carefully preserved so that we will be constantly reminded of his way of life. Everyone has an obligation to view them at least once during his lifetime.

"The field that he cleared is held in common. The island's inhabitants take turns tilling it, and the grain harvested on the land is divided into as many portions as there are settlements on the island. When a settlement receives its share, bread is made from it, which in turn is divided into as many pieces as there are inhabitants in that settlement. With respect and thankfulness the bread is then consumed by everyone in commemoration of the fact that we are all children of one father and therefore equal. At these very solemn feasts the oldest inhabitant of each settlement tells the story of the arrival of the first father and of his labors and teachings, enumerates the achievements of our forefathers and their praiseworthy attributes, repeats their time-honored counsel and admonitions, and recalls for us their beneficial and useful inventions. Such feasts usually end with the young people singing songs about the worthy deeds of our ancestors."

We spent the entire day at this sacred place. Xaoo received the portion of the grain for our settlement from the old man, and we made for home. On the way back Xaoo started discussing various types of government. "We are not familiar," he said, "with what you call monarchy, aristocracy, democracy, oligarchy, etc. In our society there is no 'political' authority other than that which parents naturally have over their children. Matters that go beyond the scope of the family are dealt with in a calm and amicable way by elders using powers of persuasion, not force. Men who are born the same cannot, or at least should not, have authority one over another. All men are equal. And when men join together to form a society, under certain circumstances and for the good of that society they will permit some authority to be vested either in a common assembly or in certain members of that assembly.

"We do not pay taxes. The goal of our society is the protection of property. The society as a whole is pledged to defend and preserve the property of each and every member if such a need arises. What would be the good of depriving ourselves of a part of our property? Why should we therefore exact a levy on ourselves? Instead, we have to be concerned lest there not be enough land to supply the population adequately with food. Thus the island is by law closed to immigration. We are watchful, and finally, we are careful not to provide an opportunity or opportunities for this to occur. We will leave this concern to our successors, together with the models of government and management we pass on. Divine Providence meted out the land solely in proportion to the number of creatures able to live on it."

Chapter Ten

We returned by a different road from the one on which we had come. When we were a half day away from our settlement, I noticed on the left side in the middle of a field a big pile of stones in the shape of a pyramid. I asked my teacher what this stood for.

"I will satisfy your curiosity," he replied. "That immense pile of stones has lain for several hundred harvests on the grave of one of our citizens, a man named Laongo. Laongo, either by chance or intent, abandoned his country by going to sea. He was gone for several years and was completely forgotten. Then unexpectedly he returned.

"When he was asked where he had been for such a long time, he told how he had bound several pieces of timber together and set sail. Sudden winds had driven him to a coast not far removed from ours. He discovered an uninhabited land, which he explored. When he wanted to return home, however, he found his timber boat was no longer by the shore, and so he was forced to stay there until he could make himself another raft from wood that was at hand. We found Laongo's explanation satisfactory. He returned to his home and took up farming as before. While he was gone, however, he had acquired knowledge, and he now used it to his advantage, infecting his fellow Nipuans with 'truths' foreign to them.

"Laongo had been paid by foreigners to destroy us. On the sly he began to tell our young people about comforts, wealth, and the joys of living extravagantly. The secret poison began to spread. The novelty of it blinded our unwary young people. He criticized Nipuan ways, making them seem crude and uncivilized—the way they appeared to you when you first came. He expounded the creature comforts of foreign nations, comforts unknown to us, which were the result of clever inventions, and he made our homeland seem loathsome. He praised the talents of our young people to the heavens and lamented the fact that their talents were being wasted unnecessarily, insisting that this was contrary to what he had seen in other lands.

"He then began to discuss the advantages of a monarchy, where one leader rules an entire nation. Under a monarch, he insisted, talent is rewarded because the bureaucracy and legal authorities place each person according to his abilities. A talented man might serve a single person and have a thousand others serve him. Although it might disturb him to be subservient to another, he would have the consolation of possessing authority over many others.

"By means of such fine talk he was successful in persuading several people to become his allies. The people he had spent time with abroad had bribed him with gifts. They wanted him to lead them to Nipu so that they could rule us. With utmost secrecy he began to share what he had brought back. These included special tools: some, like water, yielded a reflection and yet had the durability of stone or wood. There were also tiny stones of various colors strung together. Then there were some shiny, harmful instruments like your knife. But the most numerous items were round, flat pieces of yellow and white metal. Laongo said that they were useful in almost any situation and were held in such high esteem that the new people—whose coming he promised—considered them an indispensable commodity.

"This traitor and his adherents had formulated a plan. They secretly built a large boat, using a model Laongo had brought back with him, which they intended to sail to the foreigners' land, with their ringleader at the helm. Fortunately, a Nipuan walking along the shore one night heard them conversing in the bushes about this projected journey. Astounded to hear of such a strange plan, he ran and told the elders. The latter gathered together the young people and surprised Laongo and four others on that spot. The conspirators tried to defend themselves. They were bound forcibly and brought to the settlement.

"The accomplices confessed to everything. The ringleader was stubbornly silent. The tribunal was postponed for several days. Each of the culprits was kept in a special enclosure and strictly forbidden to communicate with any of Nipu's inhabitants. Then the oldest householders from each settlement gathered to deliberate, and in accordance with the verdict handed down, the items from abroad were sealed in huge containers and brought, together with the culprits, to Laongo's field. There the loathsome containers were buried deep in the earth, and after this the culprits were stoned to death. A large number of stones was then brought to construct the memorial you now see before you.

"The elders who tried the culprits composed a song to commemorate what had happened. It contains everything I have told you as well as a set of terrifying curses on these traitors to our fatherland."

Chapter Eleven

After traveling for several days we reached home. The inhabitants of the settlement came out to meet us. They accepted the grain for the common bread with joy and respect. Three days later a great feast was held, and I was asked to come to it. The oldest man present distributed the forefather's bread but did not include me. Noticing this, my host asked that I be allowed to participate, inasmuch as I was already a fellow citizen. The elder, perplexed, observed that it was not appropriate to give me a portion of the food, since I was not a son of the common father. To this Xaoo responded: "If our forefather had seen someone pass by who was hungry, would he have begrudged the passerby a piece of his bread?"

Xaoo's argument prevailed. The elder shared his own piece of bread with me, and in consuming this precious fragment I became a member of this happy family.

When everyone had eaten his fill, the young people got up and formed a circle around the elders. The most venerable elder then began to speak:

"One era provides memories to those that follow; the lessons of one day are passed on to the next. Now that we have eaten the bread of our common forefather, let us lend an ear to his admonitions.

"God is the source of all existence. God is the origin of all good. God should be the sole aim and purpose of our lives and of all our activities.

"Be kind, respectful, and obedient to parents. Parents, if you expect gratitude from your children, show your own parents gratitude.

"We are all descendants of one father; never lose sight of the fact that we are all brothers.

"Educate the young in the school of virtue.

"Virtue's greatest reward is the inner conviction it provides. Seek not other rewards. When you punish offenders, pity the offender and remember that you too are capable of sin."

He then told the story of how the forefather arrived by sea from a distant land and how he went inland to till the soil, how he built a house, reared and educated his offspring and his off-spring's offspring properly, and by means of his own sacred example laid the foundation for the general happiness of the land. After this he enumerated the virtues and the accomplishments of the common father's worthy heirs and told why they deserved to be remembered forever and ever.

Our chronicles contain great eulogies to warriors who eradi-cated whole nations, to monarchs who punished petty criminals but are honored for great crimes they themselves committed, to sages who presented their clever dreams as pronouncements, and to lawyers who contrived subtly to make the unbearable yoke of bondage seem light. We celebrate the Alexander who made half the world unhappy and also the Julius who destroyed his own fatherland. The citizens of Nipu weighed the merits of their fore-bears on a different set of scales.

One forebear they remembered with great respect had improved agricultural implements. Another had discovered the effectiveness of certain herbs in curing disease. Yet another composed the songs honoring the Supreme Being sung by the entire nation. It would take a long time to name all the forebears so honored. Suffice it to say that each was remembered eternally because of his service to society, the special respect he had shown his parents, his good upbringing, and his exemplary behavior toward fellow Nipuans.

This nation of good people, convinced that righteous deeds cannot be enhanced by rhetoric, was able to laud virtue merely by recalling those deeds. Emotions filled the righteous hearts of the young people listening. Venerable tears—a sacred consolation to an untainted conscience—flowed down the cheeks of the solemn elders. Witnessing a scene so exemplary, I was overcome with joy and admiration.

The following day, citing the forefather's maxim that youth must be educated in the school of virtue, I asked Xaoo to be so kind as to explain how one learns virtue in such a school.

"No ingenious science is taught there," he said. "Cognitive reasoning is unknown to us: we incline the heart to virtue. And to achieve this we separate the inculcation of good behavior into four stages.

"The first stage does not involve the pupil, but only the teacher. The teacher acquires a thorough understanding of his pupil's inclinations and learns how to plumb the depths of the pupil's heart, and how his pupil thinks. He also learns how the humors, the blood, along with other attributes and effects of temperament, are responsible for the pupil's health and disposition. I am sure you remember the analogy I drew earlier to the soil, how a farmer must get to know his land before he can understand how and when to plow it and what to sow in it. In much the same way we feel that a thorough knowledge of the child is needed before education can begin. After this the teacher has to decide whether gentle admonition, entertaining discourse, basic intellectual persuasion, frequent repetition, the promise of rewards, the notion of honor, or, failing all else, fear of punishment will have the best effect on the pupil's mind so that he will learn to recognize that which is good.

"The goal of the second stage is the extirpation of the evil tendencies that the teacher perceives in the pupil. No matter how hard one tries, certain faults and prejudices are instilled at infancy. Inevitably there is weakness in parents' love. Although moderated by reason, at times their love is irrational. Little by little their caresses foster stubbornness and an overly positive image of self; the child becomes restive, develops an aversion to work, and is haughty. The teacher strives to overcome these faults, for they are most easily nipped in the bud.

"In the third stage the teacher sows good grain in land that has been cleared and cultivated. Since virtue is revered, various types of virtue are described. The duties and responsibilities of each type of work are explained. No attempt is made to conceal the unpleasant aspects of leading a virtuous life. In this way young people are given due warning. When they have to perform unpleasant and arduous tasks they do not take offense.

"The fourth and last stage of an education in virtue is founded on prudence. The pupil must not merely know how to define virtue, he must also be able to achieve virtue, know how to practice it and when. At the same time, he must understand that everything has a reasonable limit. Great daring, for example, must not turn into impudence, undue caution into fear and laziness, and so forth and so on.

"These principles govern the education of our youth. Although simple, they have proven to be effective.[73]

"In addition, there are principles, vital ones, that have to do solely with the health and strength of the body. They but complement the aforementioned principles. From earliest childhood we train the children to dispense with clothing so that their bodies are inured to extreme cold and heat. For strength, they lift weights, depending on size, weight, and sex. For speed there is competitive racing. In order to learn how to cross rivers, they swim in ponds.

"Wrestling might be a good way to increase children's strength, but that type of exercise is forbidden. We are opposed to anything that resembles battle. We do not wish to give victors an opportunity to swagger, nor do we want the defeated to feel humiliated. More often than not games of this sort end in fights; they kindle hatred in those whose happiness is founded on mutual love. And people will love one another as long as they have neither reason nor cause to be envious."

Chapter Twelve

Our trip afforded me an opportunity to praise our custom of touring foreign countries. "Travel informs and enlightens our young men," I said. "They acquaint themselves with laws and customs of different nations and with various types of people. When they return, they put what they have learned to good use for the benefit of their own country."

He listened patiently to my praise and defense of what we consider the final stage in a young man's education. When I finished, he gave the following response:

"We certainly understand that travel to foreign countries can be greatly beneficial. I would not take issue with this, nor would I deny what you say. Nonetheless, you neglected to mention the harm this practice engenders. Let me quickly add, however, that in situations such as this, we normally render judgment only after the objections and opposing arguments have been weighed on the scale of reason. When more good than harm is evident, we are ready to accept advice that will benefit us. We fear that which is new, even against favorable odds. Most important to us is the certainty that comes from a lack of change in our circumstances. We are quite content with what we have. Desiring little, we need little, for those who are easy to please find contentment.

"Your taste for luxury makes you restless. Not able to make do with what you have and what you see, and unable to stay put, you constantly pursue happiness as if it were about to slip away. No matter how you justify your actions, this is the real reason you travel to foreign countries. Indeed, I have even heard you justify your trips abroad not merely on the basis of the benefits they bring but because of the fact that they are customary. Nonetheless they are vain and perhaps harmful as well.

"The greatest incentive for travel, you say, is the study of customs. Clothes do not make the man. Cap, turban, and felt hat adorn the wise and the stupid, the dishonest and the virtuous equally well. No matter what group or what society you belong to, you need not go far to find various types of people. If you closely observe the behavior of your compatriots, you will find a microcosm of the entire world. Man is fundamentally the same everywhere. Differences that result from social order, the atmosphere, or religion will not alter man's basic nature in any significant way.

"You note that these pilgrimages serve to polish the intellect. In previous discussion you said this was analogous to metal shedding rust when it is rubbed frequently. If you extend this analogy further, you will be forced to admit that the brighter the metal shines, the *smaller* it becomes.

"I do not know if it is useful for man to know many things, for then too many thoughts and imaginary things spin in his head, which the mind can barely absorb. All too often excessive mental fecundity overwhelms the intellect, and it cannot decide what to concentrate on.

"If things are worse with my neighbor than with me, is not a visit to him in vain? If things are better there, what is the point of my making a trip to find this out? For in so doing, my respect for what I have will suffer. Indeed, I will want to improve my lot without having the means to do so. I may be more enlightened, but I will be less content. Such wanderings take time and are harmful to society. For when you go away, one part of society is removed, a part useful to the whole. I hardly need mention the expense of these pilgrimages. The poorer the nation, the greater the costs. Moreover, if a nation has nothing to attract foreigners as visitors, the costs are not repaid.

"You probably will respond that you visit other lands to observe and bring back that which will benefit your compatriots. Does that mean that you will fail to see what is bad there? And do you think you will not bring back bad things too? The perfidious lure of evil preys on the human spirit. Its overt flattery has greater appeal than the strict and rigid nature of virtuous maxims.

"I would have had much more to say if I had chosen to talk about the evils of thirsting for the new and the unknown. If you think that ever-changing sights will satisfy your curiosity and calm your feelings of restlessness, you are mistaken. In the normal course of events, the more human passions are gratified, the more inflamed they become.

"Finally, kindly note if my remarks are not borne out by your own experience. You are far away from both homeland and home, and doubtless you are nostalgic. You gave up everything you had in order to satisfy your restless urges. Had you not enjoyed the special benevolence and consideration of the Supreme Being, your curiosity would have cost you your life, as it did the lives of your companions."

Chapter Thirteen

One morning when we were on our way to work in the field, one of the islanders intercepted us. Placing his hand over his heart, he said: "Father, I must complain about a neighbor..."

Without permitting him to utter another word, Xaoo asked: "Have you warned your neighbor that you were thinking of complaining?"

"I have," he replied.

Xaoo then said, "Summon him."

The islander went away and in a short while returned with the neighbor. The accuser spoke first: "I have not been in a certain part of my woodlot for two harvests. A stream separates my woodlot and field from the farm of my worthy neighbor. Yesterday, I went to that part of the woodlot to find a tree from which to fashion a new plough. When I got there, I discovered that, because of recent flooding, a little dam of mine had been washed away and the stream had changed course. It now cut off a large corner of my woodlot, including that section of land where the tree stood for which I had come. So I forded the stream and began to dig and pry the tree loose so I could fell it. My dear neighbor who was haying in his meadow noticed this. He came over to me and said: 'Fair-minded neighbor of mine! You are trespassing on my property. I would gladly give you what you desire, but I am obliged, as well you know, to preserve this property in its entirety for the good of my children. Since the brook marks the boundary between our farms, you must not use anything on this side of it without asking my permission.'

"In defense of my stand, I told him that I had the same obligation to protect and pass on property to my progeny. 'Our two properties are equal. The fact that yours has increased because the stream has been diverted does not give you a right to land that is mine.' He replied that this was a matter of interest not only to us, but to the entire settlement. We did not have the authority, he observed, to resolve it but would have to have recourse to the elders. And until they rendered judgment, it was only right that neither of us use that land. I agreed that this was right and proper, and now I turn to you, as an elder, to settle this matter in a way both fitting and conclusive."

Xaoo patiently listened to everything that was said. He asked the neighbor if everything his accuser had said was pertinent and accurate. The neighbor said that nothing had been omitted. Xaoo then said to them both: "Tomorrow I will summon the elders of the settlement. The matter will be debated, and we will decide together how to resolve it. In the morning you will both come to the Judicial Knoll for this purpose."

They went away, leaving us in the field.

I marveled when I thought about what had happened. The man who had brought the complaint not only presented his case modestly, but he also spoke of his opponent with goodwill and respect, calling him a worthy, kind, and just-minded neighbor, etc. This remarkable good-naturedness was quite different from the opening arguments in our court cases, which customarily are filled with acrimonious phrases and slander. What also amazed me was the fact that the matter under dispute was presented by only one side. This contrasted with our practice of having a lively exchange with rejoinders on both sides. Here the defendant heard out his adversary and then rested his case on the truth of the straightforward description by that adversary. The judge also was satisfied with information that came from only one source.

I asked Xaoo subsequently whether this was the way all cases were argued on Nipu. He replied in the affirmative, observing that he could see no reason why both sides should need to prattle on about a single problem. When people disagreed about something, the cause of their disagreement needed only to be presented in a straightforward manner. Those practiced in the ways of virtue and truth should have no trouble determining which side was right and resolving the matter themselves. If, on the other hand, special circumstances were involved and those concerned were not confident of their own judgment, then the elders would hear the case and have the final say.

"In our boundary disputes," I said, "if neither side possesses a written land survey, oaths are taken. The side that invokes God's name when stating its case wins."

"You godless people!" Xaoo cried out. "You dare revile the Supreme Being in this way?"

"That is not what we think," I said. "The man who swears honestly glorifies God."

I could not, however, conceal from Xaoo the fact that the practice of oath-taking is rife with abuse. I confessed that the oaths taken by those appointed to public office are largely ceremonial, that oaths designed to protect boundaries are sworn without inward conviction, and that oaths taken in connection with criminal cases are so numerous that they are of little value. The same holds true of oaths taken by those paid to support a case in court. Oaths of loyalty to the *res publica,* I informed him, are the weakest of all.

In a display of virtuous fervor, he bade me be silent. Raising his eyes and hands toward heaven, he cried out: "Blessed be those sacred hands that crushed Laongo and his accomplices with stones! The outlanders he summoned would have taught us to commit the crimes you describe. Because of what I have learned, I am doubly grateful to the Supreme Being for providing us with safeguards against your society. If you wish to give us compelling evidence of your goodwill, do not reveal the customs of your country to our people. Do not offend the sensibilities of the innocent with stories of things that would be very hard for them to believe."

The next morning I went to the Judicial Knoll, where the elders had assembled. After Xaoo had spoken in detail about the property in dispute, they all proceeded to the place in question and examined everything closely. The elders then ordered the entire community to restore the original course of the stream, build a stronger dam, and shore up the banks so that they would not give way again. As was customary in these situations, the elders were thanked by both sides, and the accuser invited his opponent to a feast.

Chapter Fourteen

There were many other customs and teachings preserved from time immemorial on this island. To enumerate them all would make my story too long, so I will mention only a few briefly.

Nipuans learn the history of their country not only from stories recounted by elders at banquets but also from songs that celebrate the deeds and most significant experiences of their ancestors. Nipuan poetry is less sonorous than ours and lacks its grace. The simple yet dignified quality of this verse, however, more than compensates for its lack of adornment. Compositions about love or ones containing indecent expressions are unknown. All their songs seek to praise the virtuous life, condemn transgressions, and damn transgressors.

On Nipu the year is measured by the solar cycle. Years are reckoned by harvests. If they had any notion of eras, I was unaware of it. When, or how long ago, the forefather arrived was also not known. Xaoo, who did not look more than, say, fifty, reckoned that he was ninety-two. On Nipu it is not unusual for men to reach the age of one hundred twenty.

Since they know nothing about metals, the Nipuans fashion farming implements from the bones of large fish that are thrown up by the sea on their shores. Rubbing one bone against another makes the bones sharp enough for carpentry as well as reaping.

On the first day of the new moon Nipuans rest. The elders pay one another visits to discuss matters of common interest. The young people go out into the fields and engage in various types of athletic contests. The games are all designed to build strength and vigor. Members of both sexes participate as equals, and there are always elders and gray-haired matrons present to prevent any offense to modesty and probity.

I did not see a single musical instrument that resembled ours. Nipuans dance to songs set to dance rhythms and sung.

Some of their songs resemble our dramas. When, for example, the Nipuans portray the deeds of their forebears, they have people play the forebears in the song. And when the person represented is supposed to speak, the player sings and conveys by gestures that person's inner emotions or actions. Others do the same for the forebears they represent. The chorus sings the narrative portion, as well as intoning moral reflections, paeans to virtue, and curses against transgressors.

The Nipuans do not eat the flesh of animals or fish. Xaoo preferred not to believe that we subsist on this form of nourishment.

Since the practice of consuming meat is scorned, the Nipuans know nothing of hunting, and the island's fauna is very tame. Nipuans know nothing of the existence of lions, tigers, and wolves. The roe deer and hare that I saw there were somewhat different from those we have in Europe and very few in number. Cows and oxen are abundant. They are raised in cow barns and used both for work in the fields and for milk production. Nipuan wool is wonderfully beautiful and soft. The sheep are shorn twice a year, and from the wool the women weave the fabric from which clothing, quilts, and mattresses are made.

One marries for life. It was so difficult for Xaoo to comprehend polygamy that I could not convince him that it was actually practiced. He took it for granted that the number of wives and husbands was a matter mutually agreed on. When he learned that this privilege was extended only to men, he got angry at the injustice of it all.

The complexities of law and the deceit of judges could not find a foothold on Nipu. The Nipuans live in blissful ignorance of legal systems that, they would tell us, were invented not for our good but for the suppression of truth and the justification of heinous crimes.

Chapter Fifteen

One day, while walking near the place where I had been cast ashore after being shipwrecked, I pondered my fate at some length. I recalled all the events in my life; I was not completely certain whether my present situation was advantageous.

My thoughts kept changing, stirring up my imagination even more than had the vivid pictures of the past. On the bank, under a protruding rock, I caught sight of a fairly large portion of a wrecked ship that strong waves had thrust onto the sandy shore. It had been left high and dry when the sea retreated. The wreck was in a secluded spot, so I was not afraid that someone would see me if I approached it quickly. I went up to it and found that the stern of the ship had been preserved. I knew that this was where the captain's quarters were usually located and where the most valuable items on board ship were stored.

I was able to force my way into the cabin and found many objects there. Anything dampness could spoil had completely rotted. Other things, such as pistols and rifles, were covered with rust but could be made serviceable again. I feasted my eyes on this unexpected discovery. To keep the local people from finding what I had discovered, I looked for a cache under a nearby rock. I found a sizable cave in a place that could not be easily seen and diligently hauled my booty there.

I had gathered up nearly everything before I noticed in one corner of the captain's cabin a compartment concealed in the flooring whose cover was coming loose. I tore the cover off, and for the first time in three years the gleam of gold caught my eyes. Although it was of no value on this island, fond memories of all the former uses of this metal so fired my imagination that I experienced a feeling of great joy. I could tell from the stamp of the mint that they were louis d'or, and I carried them off quickly to the cave. By then the sun had already begun to dip toward the west. To keep the Nipuans from thinking that I had been delayed and wondering why, I made for the settlement as fast as I could.

I did not sleep a wink that night. Realizing that I was the possessor of no small treasure, I regretted over and over that I was in a place where it would do me no good. In my mind's eye I pictured myself at home in Poland, buying up villages and towns, building palaces, and laying out gardens. But there was sadness in my joy because what fate had spitefully bestowed on me with beguiling and deceitful caresses was in fact of no use.

The following day, as soon as the sun had risen, I went to Xaoo and told him that I was suffering from a severe headache and proposed that I spend the day trying to rid myself of it by means of strict diet and physical exercise. He readily agreed. Taking some food with me, I ran with the speed of light to my booty. Before examining the things I had concealed in the cave (I checked first to make certain they had not been disturbed), I went back to the wreck and searched every corner of it for additional items. In one corner I discovered a case. Unnailing the lid, inside I found quite a few books that had not yet rotted from the moisture. I also found in the wreck a keg of gunpowder and a pouch with balls and shot.

I hauled these valuable items to my cave and ventured further along the bank to make certain that no one was spying on me. As I did so, I noticed a few leagues away on the shore a boat, undoubtedly one from the ship. In it were two oars and nothing more. I brought it to the mouth of a nearby stream. Using a rope I had taken from the ship, I tied the boat to a tree in a spot that was shielded completely from the eyes of the curious by thick brushwood.

Returning to the cave, I was able to examine my riches calmly for the first time. I began with the casket and pouches containing money. I found 4,862 double and 3,716 single French ducats in gold. In addition, a special compartment in the casket contained several dozen large, uncut diamonds and several hundred small ones, as well as a large number of semiprecious stones, rubies, emeralds, and sapphires.

By good fortune, water had not found its way into the casket, so I was also able to retrieve several small bundles of records. These I took with me; I wanted to read them carefully at home. Since the books were partially soaked, I removed them from the case and spread them out on the sand to dry. The other items I salvaged were two rifles, three pairs of pistols, and four swords; two spyglasses that had been so thoroughly soaked that they were unusable; a speaking trumpet for communicating with other ships; three gold watches, one with a striking mechanism; a silver vase, six serving dishes, and twenty plates; seven wire cages (it was clear from the remaining feathers that there had been parrots in them); a box that must have been for wigs, judging from all the hair, congealed pomade, and odor of bergamot oil, not to mention the curling irons (two of them, one for trimming toupees) found in it; three violins, which were ruined, a lute, two pairs of clarinets, and one French horn; a small wooden box *de mahoni* with brass trim containing twelve bottles of lavender water; and forty-two pounds of tobacco *de Marocco* that had been utterly ruined.

The remaining items—namely, clothing and linen—had been

destroyed by the seawater. There were also paintings, but the paint had peeled off, and it was impossible to tell what might have been depicted on them.

Chapter Sixteen

My "ailment" lasted a second day. Under the same pretext, I supplied myself with food and hurried back to my treasure. I learned from the records that the wrecked vessel had belonged to a ship-owner in the French city of Saint-Malo. Among the records I found various drafts for money, one for redemption in Amsterdam in the amount of 12,000 ducats, another for redemption in London in the amount of 22,000 ducats, and three for redemption in Genoa, each in the amount of 6,500 ducats. I did not discard this booty, because I thought it might come in handy at some point, but put it with the gold.

To keep my walks from rousing suspicion, I decided to let Xaoo know that I had seen a section of a wrecked ship from Europe. To prevent him from realizing that I had already taken things out of it, I returned one of the rifles, two rusty pistols, the musical instruments, and the case of books—now all dry—to the captain's quarters. The books I brought back deliberately. I thought that by interpreting them to Xaoo I could give him a sense of our accomplishments in various areas of learning. Things went just as I had planned.

Xaoo, it turned out, was more interested in preventing his fellow Nipuans from suffering potentially harmful consequences than he was in indulging his own curiosity. At the break of dawn he went with me to see what was left of the wrecked ship. He examined every part of it closely, inquiring about the purpose and use of everything he saw. He threw the rifles and pistols into the ocean after I explained how they were used. He allowed me to take the books home; the instruments we left in the ship.

The following day before I woke, Xaoo and the elders went

and burned what remained of the ship. Xaoo woke me and told me what they had done when he came back. Since he spoke in general terms about a boat, I was terribly afraid at first that they had found the one I had left hidden in the brushwood by the shore. Then he asked me to explain the content of the books that had been on the ship. I promised to do so after I had had time to examine them thoroughly.

This I started to do. Since all the books were in French, they were easy for me to understand. I will not list them; it has been so long that I do not remember all the titles. I do recall finding Molière's comedies, thirty-eight romances, four books about political economy, a large collection of arias *de l'Opéra comique*, an edition of Anacreon with copperplate engravings, volume 3 of Newton's *Philosophiae*, a recipe book for pâtés, and four maps of Paris.

In a few days Xaoo begged me to tell him something about the books' content. To explain the charm of Anacreontic verse to an inhabitant of Nipu would be difficult and, what is more, inappropriate. The contrast with the local songs was simply too great. Since Nipuans could not imagine lying in a refined way, I had to forget about the romances. Among people not well versed in music the opera arias would have commanded little respect. The philosophy of Newton, on the other hand, was something I myself did not understand. I proceeded therefore to Molière. Drawing an analogy with Nipuan songs, I explained comedy to him, saying that comedy teaches good morals by entertaining people, that comedy presents human beings in their most natural form, and that in comedy virtue always prevails and vice, once exposed, is doomed.

"Our laws prevent crime through the threat of punishment," I said. "We learn all our social responsibilities from the gentle yet firm admonitions of our own elders. Comedy has an equally firm and perhaps even more effective way of making transgressors seem repugnant: it ridicules them. More often than not the results obtained are better than those of more 'serious' methods. Scorn is particularly offensive to one's amour propre. This is why ridicule—provided of course that it is honest and restrained—is so effective."

To reinforce what I had said, I proceeded to translate one of

Molière's comedies. Since I wanted to make Xaoo understand how severely the rigorous maxims of Molière judge us, I chose *Le Misanthrope*.

It took me several days to finish the translation. After I had read it to him, he said: "The man who wrote this composition must have known people very well. Human passion is well portrayed, and a fine example of great eccentricity of character is given. It seems to me, however, that the author overlooked several things in his work. First of all, by making his recluse virtuous, is he not implying that virtue is by nature repugnant? In permitting indiscreet and premature criticisms to fall from the lips of the virtuous misanthrope, he deprives him of virtue's most valuable attribute, discernment. Moreover, by having him oppose even innocuous social customs, he gives the misanthrope an inflated sense of self-esteem.

"My son, true virtue is characterized differently. An honest man will sense that his actions are not like those of other men, but this will not make him conceited. To him the company of vicious people is inherently repugnant, but he does not avoid such people, especially when he can set a good example. He does not put on airs, because he does not want to make himself repugnant. When he can, he mitigates the unpleasant aspects of obligations, aspects that at first glance may seem quite severe. He does this to keep men in the fold whose minds vacillate between good and evil. Perhaps you intended to draw a subtle analogy between the speeches of the misanthrope and my own. I cannot take offense at this because I know you are not yet fully accustomed to our ways. Please note well that, in accordance with our time-honored views and firmly rooted system of safeguards, *you* are to us peculiar, not I to you. It is my duty to make you adapt to our ways. When you and I discuss the bad habits of those people in whose midst you were born and reared, I must use the most effective means available. If I were to come and live with your people, I would not wish to stand out in any way. I would blindly follow your example as long as doing so did not alter my basic sense of responsibility. However, if this meant that virtue had to be sacrificed, I confess that I would rather shun society and behave like an eccentric, recluse, and misanthrope than be fashionable but dishonest."

Chapter Seventeen

The ancients were right when they spoke of the "sweet smoke" of one's native land.[74] The sight of things from Europe awakened in me the desire to return. The gold, though valueless on Nipu, had utterly beguiled me. I became greedy without hope of profit, and I felt anxious while enjoying complete security. The considerable fortune I possessed made me constantly restless. I would formulate plans, estimate profits, ponder the value of my goods. But when I stopped and thought about the impossibility of realizing any of my plans on this island, I fell into deep despair. I lamented that fate had made a plaything of me, giving me means I could not put to use.

I had actually grown accustomed to the Nipuan way of life. I had begun to value the sacred tranquillity of the place. But that metal known as gold was not content to make me miserable in Europe alone; it now pursued me the world over. I struggled constantly with myself. I kept reminding myself that there was no way to profit from the gold, that it was impossible to leave Nipu, and that even if I could, I would do so at the risk of exposing myself to new dangers and being ungrateful to my benefactors.

Thoughts such as these were quite convincing to my mind, but my heart knew otherwise. I was ready to make a heroic sacrifice: I would throw the gold and all the other things from Europe into the sea. When I took some of the pouches out of the cave with this in mind, however, the thought of doing so filled me with repugnance. I realized that it was impossible to subdue my desire for change. So I resolved to leave the island in the boat I had salvaged from the wrecked ship, even though I was almost certain that this would bring about my ruin.

Xaoo noticed my great agitation. I attributed it to my impaired health. I did this primarily so that, under the pretext of going for a walk, I could visit my treasure more often.

The story Xaoo had told about Laongo strengthened my belief that Nipu was located not far from other inhabited lands. Moreover, from what I had been told about the gifts Laongo had been given, I was certain there must be European settlements there.

So I kept returning to my boat. In the course of making it shipshape, I discovered that it had not been damaged in any way. I gave it a mast and sewed sails. I also readied the oars.

I divided the boat into three sections: one to hold provisions, another for water in kegs, and the third for utensils and my treasure. I made a special place for the gunpowder. I also got the rifles and pistols ready for use. I worked so diligently that it took only a few days to prepare everything.

I was extremely sorry that the ship's compass had been ruined so that I could not use it to navigate. Forced to conjecture which way to sail, I decided it would be best to follow a westerly course. For as far as I could determine, our ship had sailed consistently from the east and had not sighted land for twenty-six days. Hence I calculated that the settlements Laongo had discovered were to be found in the opposite direction.

One morning, as usual, I went to my boat but found that it was missing. All my utensils, valuables, provisions, and ammunition were stowed in it. To this day I recognize that, had Divine Providence not intervened at that moment, I would have died then and there or jumped into the sea out of despair. I stood as if rooted to the spot and so remained for some time. Returning to my senses, I began to shed bitter tears. It did not take me long to realize how useless grief was under the circumstances, and I started to walk along the stream toward the sea. Suddenly I caught sight of my boat; it had gone out with the tide. I hurled myself into the sea and swam to it. Fearing that this might happen again, when favorable winds came up I decided to set sail.

End of Book Two

BOOK THREE

Chapter One

I was so filled with the hope of seeing my native land again and so satisfied by the change in circumstances that I forgot about my present danger. A favorable wind drove my boat, and I sat quietly, lost in thought. Some time later, when I looked back and saw the shores of Nipu sinking in the distance, I realized, as if waking from a dream, how impudent I had been in leaving. The thought that I had lost the companionship of such honest people made my heart ache. The copious tears I shed—genuine tears, since they were shed not for others to see—were a worthy tribute to Nipuan virtue and proof of my gratitude for the many good things the Nipuans had done for me.

Had these feelings been stronger, they would have triumphed over my longing to see Poland, since that was but a slim possibility, and I undoubtedly would have turned back. In the end, however, it was the appeal of new adventures rather than love of country that prevailed. Losing all sight of the land I had forsaken, I lost the desire to return. I was completely on my own, the captain, coxswain, and sailor of my ship. Toward evening, when I had eaten something and sensed that a gentle sleep was gradually closing my weary lids, I commended myself to fate, no, rather to that Force that does not forsake those who trust in it, Divine Providence.

When I opened my eyes the next day, the sun was already near the middle of its diurnal course. I looked about on all sides, hoping to see a shore or a boat under sail, but to no avail. The spyglass I had more or less mended presented me with nothing all around except the sadly monotonous expanse of the sea. A second day of favorable winds saved me effort. Nonetheless, thoughts whirled around ceaselessly in my head. Some were comforting, but others caused me to feel sorrow and fear. That strong desire to see my native land—my original impulse—passed, and longing for the inhabitants of Nipu whom I had forsaken returned, growing ever stronger.

I sailed eight days in whatever direction the winds blew me. By the ninth day the provisions were already significantly depleted, the water was beginning to taste foul, and I was in a constant state of anxiety and sought a shore or boat every moment. By the eleventh day I noticed my strength weakening substantially. The provisions, now both meager and spoiled, no longer fortified me. Filled with despair, I was assailed by the thought that I should act boldly and resolutely in order to escape prolonged torture. But that same ray of hope, that same fortifying Assurance that stayed my hand after the shipwreck, now dispersed the darkness of my folly and permitted the salutary light of religion to enter. When night came, though I strained to fall asleep, I could not because of the turbulence inside me. I impatiently awaited daybreak. This would certainly be the last day of my life.

The sunrise, dear to every creature, gave me cause for sorrow. At the sight of this pleasant, but last, dawn, I began to cry bitterly. Only one day's provisions remained. And although I might survive a few days without eating, I was so weak that I did not expect to last until the following day. With the little strength I had left I hung a large piece of white linen from the wrecked ship atop the mast. I hoped a passing boat would sight it and raise me, perhaps unconscious, from the depths. No longer able to stand on my feet, I lay down in the middle of the boat to await my final destiny.

Chapter Two

The sun was beginning to set. I had just about exhausted my strength and was feeling much like a sleepwalker, when I thought

I heard the sound of a cannon being fired in the distance. Assuming this to be the result of an overstrained imagination, I paid it no heed. When I heard the same sound repeated more forcefully, I rose up and, without the aid of my spyglass, saw a large ship approaching.

When a voice emanating from a speaking trumpet reached my ears, I knew how someone condemned to death and brought to the public square must feel upon hearing that mercy will be shown and his sentence remitted. I was being ordered to come alongside, I gathered, for the language was not one I understood. I grabbed an oar, but my hands were so weak that it dropped out of them. This was noted, and a boat was immediately launched. When it came close, I surmised from the dress of the people that they must be Spaniards. I was put into their boat, and my boat was brought close to the ship. My things were taken aboard, and the boat was then left to drift.

From the outset I observed that the captain was a haughty, severe person who did not mince words. He ordered me taken below and fed. I could barely chew the hard biscuit I was given, but the goblet of wine, something I had not tasted for several years, had the effect of a cordial. When I felt like getting out of bed and said I wanted to thank the captain for his help and also collect my things, my attendant told me in French that the captain's orders were not to let me leave the cabin until my things had been thoroughly examined.

I was alarmed by the thought of what I might lose as a result of such a search. Pleased, however, to be alive, I hid my anxiety and begged my attendant to tell me something of the ship and of the people I was with. He confirmed my initial conjecture that the ship was Spanish. It was returning to America with slaves rounded up in Africa for work in the gold mines of Potosí. The captain was one Don Emanuel Alvarez y Astorgas y Bubantes. We were only five days away from the shores of Mexico, assuming the winds remained favorable.

I spent the remainder of the day resting in the little cabin, fearful that some misadventure still lay in store for me. Sweet sleep calmed me. About noon of the next day I woke feeling hale and hearty. To my surprise, there was still no decision whatsoever from the captain. At the very moment I was worrying about this matter, the door opened, and several soldiers came in. They pulled me out of bed and put my legs in fetters. I tried to defend myself, but the strength and agility of these ruffians were too great for me. Without knowing what was happening, I let them take me where they wished.

They took me down to the bottom of the ship, fastened me to a long chain in a dark and smelly place, and left me there half alive. At first I paid no heed to where they had put me. There was a medley of voices speaking in unfamiliar tongues. Bitter sobs and groans, however, put an end to my apathy. Examining closely my wretched companions, I could tell, despite the darkness of the place, that I was among the Negroes being taken to work in the mines. I tried to find out if any of them spoke a language I knew, but no one understood me. I tried using Nipuan; this too was unknown to them. Crying and groaning were the only sounds any of them made. I helped them in every way I could. Toward evening, when food was brought, the guard gave me half a moldy biscuit. As drink we shared a few buckets of spoiled water.

Chapter Three

During the horrible time I spent in the boat, it never once occurred to me that there could be a worse fate in store. The cannon shots that I thought signaled life had in fact condemned me to misery. Death, which I escaped as if by miracle, now seemed like the calmest of harbors after tumultuous seas. I was nourished by tears. And the despair, which at first agitated me greatly, now made me forgetful and callous.

After a few days I rallied somewhat. Intense grief replaced the despair and callousness. An uncontrollable thought kept troubling me: What turn would my fate take next? Although convinced that I was being taken to mine ore in the bowels of the earth, a strange inner voice now and again repeated that I would not have to do this for long. My spirits were also raised by the thought that I had sewn into a scapular on my chest the drafts salvaged from the wrecked ship. Herein lay a plan for my deliverance. I hoped that a compassionate person would visit our subterranean abode. I would guarantee him a substantial reward if he would cash one of the drafts and redeem me with the money.

It was easy to guess that the captain's greed had caused my misfortune. Undoubtedly he wanted to profit from the treasure that had come his way, and to do so he had to tell his crew that he had learned from my papers that I belonged to a band of pirates or that I was one of those who trafficked in contraband. When I thought of my flight from Nipu, I decided that what had happened to me was fit retribution for the ingratitude I had shown. This thought gave me strength, and I became determined to endure my misfortune with all the patience I could muster. I would try to profit from the ordeal cruel fate had visited upon me.

Thus I have to admit that the position I now found myself in constituted the finest "school" of my life. What Xaoo had not proved to me, Spanish shackles did. I learned that one should be content with one's lot and not search for happiness armed with fanciful plans and projects. Capricious thoughts, I learned, produce inner turbulence and bring bad results. Finally, I learned how inordinate desire for wealth blinds one to need and leads to poverty.

I spent the entire voyage, a voyage protracted because of fickle winds, in reflections of this sort. Hunger, various annoyances, and fatigue resulting from the many hardships took their daily toll among the worn-out slaves. When we anchored along the coast of Spanish America, fewer than a third were reckoned fit for work.

We came into a port, where we spent a short time before being taken to Potosí. The sight of the New World assuaged me more than anything else. Everything was unusual: animals, birds, trees, herbs, and fruit. Everything was different from what we know, and all of it seemed superior.

Chapter Four

It is generally thought that imagination magnifies our fears because it is subject to so little control. When I first entered the caverns of Potosí, I realized that this notion was not without exception. The place was horrible, a living hell. The state of the toiling slaves was more wretched than that of animals; the supervisors were cruel as well as severe. Although prepared to endure, when pushed alive into this grave I was totally revolted.

Like it or not, I had to start to work. Still young and strong, I was indeed able to fulfill the arduous tasks of mining. I tried, as best I could, to do everything I was ordered to do. I did not manage, however, to soften the steel heart of the overseer by being obedient. His piercing voice echoed in the subterranean pits. It was an ominous voice, one that heralded floggings of the guilty and innocent alike.

If he who thinks that gold is life's most indispensable commodity, he who expends all his energy on accumulating as much of it as possible, if only he, I say, were to realize each time he delights in this metal how much its extraction costs in human tears, he would curb his greed and spare millions of unhappy people who become victims of that greed.

Many a time, buried alive in the caves, did I recall how angry I would get at the Nipuans for calling us Europeans savages. These fine people knew only in part the reason we so justly deserve this name. The Nipuans are themselves testimony to the fact that gold does not bring happiness. The world as a whole demonstrates how the gold that gratifies the excesses of but a small part of the population makes ten people poor for every one made happy.

Unable to converse, I made efforts to learn Spanish, not a difficult endeavor for one who speaks Italian. Before long I could engage in ordinary conversation without trouble.

I noticed once among the many visitors to our caves a grayhaired American native. Later I learned that this person was a trader who owned property not far from Potosí. He visited the toiling slaves from time to time, raising their spirits with gentle words and ministering to those who were sick. Because of this everyone considered him his father. Even the supervisors respected him.

One time in passing me, the American noticed how unbelievably wretched I was. He gave me a few small coins. I accepted them gratefully. Surprised that a savage would act in such a manner (for he was from a tribe not subject to Spanish authority), I tried to get to know him better, and when he came a second time and gave me alms, I said: "What makes you pity me?"

"You are a man, just as I am," he answered.

These words, so simple yet so very wise, to my mind made him worthy of being a Nipuan. We became close friends; our conversations sweetened the bitterness of my captivity. Having developed an affection for me, he visited me more often. He told me that he belonged to a local tribe and that he had property of his own further inland.

When I described the customs and way of life on Nipu, he told me that the Nipuan settlement must have been founded at the time the Spanish were conquering America. "I am certain," he went on, "that some of our unhappy tribal leaders, escaping their own land, took to the sea and peopled this island. For what you tell me about the Nipuans accords with the character and manner of thinking of our ancient fathers. In any event, whatever may have happened and whether the Nipuans trace their origins to the American natives or to you, I see that they retain our distinctive character traits and that they truly embody the type of life we led before the arrival of the Spanish.

"In your histories it is written that the people you found here were savage, harsh, hotheaded, treacherous, and murderous. It seems to me that your authors actually modeled their definitions on themselves. Since we could not fathom what you did, we at first considered you gods or at least superior beings. When we heard the tremendous roar of your firearms, we thought that thunderbolts were being hurled at us, and we abandoned our homes and ran into the woods. For this we were branded cowards by the Europeans.

"By nature we are inclined to be kind, but we also tend to be impulsive. What occurred, therefore, is what occurs to any kind people who are made to feel desperate: we wreaked excessive vengeance and were cruel, as you Europeans recorded. He who wishes to exonerate us must put himself in our position and acknowledge that we have been deceived in the most wicked ways imaginable, robbed of everything, and tormented mercilessly in the name of treason, might, and greed and that we have yet to be fully avenged."[75]

Chapter Five

In our various discussions I had an opportunity to tell the American about all of my adventures. Eventually I begged him to think of ways to liberate me. Since I was completely convinced that the American was a kindhearted person, I plucked up my courage and confided that sizable drafts of money concealed on my person could be used for ransom. Since he did not know how to redeem such drafts, he did not dare to take this task upon himself. He did, however, promise to bring when he could a European, his friend, whose honesty he vouched for.

I waited two months for that savior, a wait so long that I had begun to be plagued by great despondency and feelings of weakness. The kind old American noticed this and visited as often as he could, cheering me with the prospect of his friend's coming. I was beginning to doubt his sincerity and to think that he had deceived me with false hope out of compassion, when he ran up to me one day with joy in his eyes, promising that he would come with the friend in a few days. Those few days seemed like ages to me.

Four days later he appeared with a person no longer young but still hale and hearty. The person's dress was extremely plain: he wore a frock of thin, gray cloth without pleats and with small buttons. On his head was a broad-brimmed hat, and his hair, gray in places, was combed back simply. Everything about him suggested order and cleanliness. When I was pointed out, the friend, Quaker William, came up to me and, without removing his hat and without any preliminary greeting, said: "Pay heed, my brother! Thou art unhappy, and I am wealthy. I shall ransom thee. And when thou art free, thou wilt tell me what thou needest, and I will give it to thee. Thank me not. Show thy gratefulness if thou so wishest. If thou choosest not to show thy thanks, I shall not be offended. If at some other time the Lord God shows thee His favor, remember to do unto others as they have done unto thee."

I tried to fall at his feet, but he angrily leapt away from me. He then proceeded to the mine superintendent and paid a sum for me three times the normal ransom paid for slaves. My shackles were removed, and the kind American, in Quaker William's stead, took me immediately to the house where he was living. There I found prepared for me clothing and the following letter:

> Brother of mine! Offer thanks to God for Thy freedom. People are mere instruments of His Providence. What Thou findest here, use wisely. Fare Thee well.

William

With the letter I found a draft for five hundred pounds sterling, worth roughly one thousand ducats. I wanted to go to William at once, but the American stopped me and said that William had gone elsewhere to attend to some business and probably would not return for two days. The draft seemed unnecessary, since I had drafts for considerable sums myself. I wanted to return the draft to William, who, the American told me, knew nothing of my wealth and thought I needed help. The American knew William well, however, and he warned me not to pain him by doing this. I made up my mind then and there that as soon as I had redeemed my drafts, I would use his money to ransom other slaves. And once I had obtained some of my money, I did precisely this.

We were unwilling to wait until William returned and went instead to the city where he lived. He received us with every imaginable kindness and invited us to stay with him in his house. Only by exercising great force did I keep myself from expressing gratitude to him for saving me. He, on the other hand, treated me as if he had absolutely no knowledge of what he had done for me.

William had bought the house in which he lived a long time ago because it was a convenient place to conduct business. It had none of the usual adornments that set the dwellings of the rich apart from those of others. There was nonetheless an abundance of all the things necessary to live an upright yet fully comfortable existence. Accompanying this was an order and neatness so exquisite that one approached even familiar objects with new respect. A whole way of thinking was reflected in the house's appearance. Although at first its peculiarities might elicit feelings of disgust, anyone able to overcome such feelings would gain insight into the finest spiritual qualities known to man.

Chapter Six

William learned from the American that I had used the five hundred pounds sterling to ransom other slaves. One day he took me aside and said: "Brother of mine! Thou art worthy of the company of honorable people. I know what thou didst with the money I gavest thee, and that comforted me. From this time on I shall regard thee as my son. Be completely open with me. Say what thou needest, and I shall provide it."

He stopped and reflected for a moment before continuing. "I understand that my conduct surprises thee—at first even offended thee—because it is so direct and unaffected. It is true that I do not speak, and probably also do not think, as custom now dictates. On the other hand, I have no desire to learn these skills, because I do not see how they can be useful. I am accustomed to doing things in a simple way. May I depart this earth a simple yet honest man. No honest man, nor any thinking being, can conceal what is dear to his heart or deceive with false appearances. I am well aware that my simplicity and that of people like me offends those who pay lip service to politeness. Is it not better to disillusion at the first meeting rather than be disillusioning as time goes on?

"I heard thy story from my friend the American. It prompted me to befriend thee. Thy unfortunate condition was itself testimony to thy need. But what made thee known to me is what thou hast just done. Thou givest me great pleasure, and I am thy friend. I know that thou wilt reciprocate. To start our friendship, tell me what thou desirest so that I might serve thee."

I tried to be as open with him as he was with me. I told him that my greatest wish now was to return to Europe, see my home-land again, settle my debts, and live once more on my ancestral estates. "And dost thou have means for this?" asked William.

I promised to show him the drafts I had found on the wrecked ship. In response he said: "Although in all likelihood the person who possessed these notes drowned, he must have heirs. Thus, in using this person's wealth, thou doest an injustice to his heirs, heirs about whom knowledge may be available. Please do not think that thou canst exercise that disgraceful right whereby ownership of things belonging to people who perish at sea passest to the finders. This practice is nothing short of savagery because it justifies robbery. A truly good-hearted person wilt not want to profit from the misfortune of another even if it is legal to do so."

William's observation dismayed me. I could not help but agree with his arguments, but I knew that if the booty were restored to its rightful owners I would be deprived of the means to pay my debts and to lead an upright life in my native country.

The following day I brought the drafts to William. He took them to his study. He was there only a short time. When he emerged, his face was merry. Clasping me by the hand, he said: "I thank God for such good fortune. That French ship was carrying my goods and drafts for money. I resigned myself long ago to the thought that I had lost it all, but if Providence hast put these things in thy hands, then I surrender them all to thee most willingly. I have been repaid for the loss at great profit in that I have been able to oblige thee. Do not think that this gift will ruin me. By the grace of God I have an abundance of everything; I was reim-bursed for this loss long before it happened."

Mindful of the American's warning, I was careful not to be profuse in my thanks. I bowed slightly to my benefactor, then hugged him heartily. With hardly a pause, William continued his speech. Having learned of my wish to return to Poland, he promised to find a way of sending me to Europe posthaste. And indeed, as soon as we came to Buenos Aires, he discovered a French ship about to return to Marseilles. He reported this to me immediately and, sighing deeply, said: "I must confess that this leave-taking is pain-ful for me. Friendship makes me want to detain thee longer, but friendship also tells me to forego pleasure and fulfill thy wish. Were I not obliged to stay here and conduct business, I would have thee return with me to Pennsylvania as a companion. I know that thou wouldst like both the country and the people. And although the virtue and innocence of thy island may be lacking, when all is said and done, thou wouldst perhaps perceive some affinities there with Nipu and the Nipuans. Thou wilt grant me, I trust, a dozen days or so. Since I must remain here several months still, I dare not thwart thy rightful and natural wish to see thy homeland.''

During the time of our sojourn in Buenos Aires William learned that the captain of the slave ship had brought his vessel into the harbor. William brought a complaint before the local court using me as a case in point. The court awarded jewelry and money to William. The lord high commissioner stripped the captain of all his prerogatives. The remaining wealth the captain had amassed by transporting slaves was confiscated, and the captain, bereft of respect, honor, and riches, was himself dispatched to the mines. And so Don Emanuel Alvarez y Astorgas y Bubantes went in my stead to Potosí.

The ship going to Marseilles would be in port only three days. During this time William and his friend the American made preparations for my trip. As the time to leave approached, I was so greatly burdened by the thought of having to say good-bye that I asked William's permission to stay. At first he was prone to honor my request, but then, expostulating on the duties of a citizen toward his homeland, he rejected it.

We went and looked the ship over two days before it was to set sail. William persuaded me to spend the night on board, promising that he and his friend would return the following day. Sadly I said good-bye. Since night was approaching, I lay down on my bunk. At first the pitching of the ship—slight, since it was at anchor—annoyed me, but eventually I fell into a deep sleep. When I awoke, the new day had already begun, and the ship seemed to be sailing under favorable winds. I leapt out of bed and peered out the window; the shores of America were no longer in sight. An unbearable feeling of sorrow gripped me; I had lost William and the American and had not even been able to bid them farewell.

Chapter Seven

Filled with sorrow, I flung myself on the bunk and sobbed. Suddenly the ship's captain appeared and, seeing how distraught I was, humored me by intimating that William, fearing his own emotions, had left quickly without saying anything to me. He then handed me a letter, which read as follows:

> Brother of mine! I spare my own feelings and Thine. In all likelihood we will never see one another again. I would have done Thee an injustice to ask Thee to remain my faithful friend. Thou knowest that I am Thy friend and sendest Thee every good wish. Accept what I offer as a reminder of our friendship. Fare Thee well.
>
> William

I shed profuse tears as I read the letter. The margrave de Vennes (the captain of the ship) announced that everything found in my quarters had been provided for my comfort and pleasure by William as a gift. The feeling of sadness, admiration, and gratitude was so great that I could not say a word.

As the margrave said, everything needed to make things comfortable and pleasurable had been provided. That outwardly simple Quaker had demonstrated that he was fully aware of the finest products available. An exquisite wardrobe had been prepared, including an ample supply of fine underlinen. The table service was plain, but in good taste. In the little compartments of the writing desk every single tiny drawer contained something distinctive. In one of those little drawers, I also found several thousand ducats carefully packed in little bundles. William had not forgotten to include a traveling library. It was not large but was well selected.

I feared this magnificent gift had been a hardship for William, but the captain, who was acquainted with William's circumstances, assured me that William was one of the wealthiest merchants in Pennsylvania with almost unlimited resources. He had helped many destitute people get back on their feet. Because he managed his affairs well and was thrifty in the proper sense of that word, he possessed a well-nigh inexhaustible source of funds to use for philanthropy.

The French are sociable by nature: the margrave's lack of formality obviated the need for those tedious declarations and ceremonies that getting acquainted customarily entails. He was young, having not yet attained the age of thirty. He was well proportioned and had a kind manner and a handsome face. His entire appearance denoted one who was wellborn, courteous, and worldly-wise. Because he was vivacious and eloquent, I cast him in the role we normally assign to a Frenchman, namely, that of a polite scatterbrain whose entire mental exertions are devoted to trifles; who does not really care for genuine feelings of friendship or of love; who mocks everything, everyone everywhere; who has an exaggerated sense of national pride; who views with disdain everything beyond the Rhine, across the sea, or over the Pyrenees; who is constant only in his own eccentricities; who follows solely the fashion of the day; and who loves no one but himself.

For this reason, therefore, I thought I should deal with the margrave in a polite but cautious manner. I would enjoy meeting with him but would be on my guard against a possible ruse. So I spent the first few days of our voyage in conversation about nothing but trifles. If I noticed that our discussion was verging toward more serious matters, matters that might require thoughtful attention, I would redirect the conversation toward ordinary things, being careful not to annoy the margrave.

One day we happened to talk about the Nipuans. I was not yet able to contain my feelings about them and was profuse in my praise. I proceeded to laud their attributes, their kindness, their customs. To extol them even more, I drew some rather vivid analogies at our expense. My speech eventually evolved to the point that no European nation was described in complimentary terms. Individual people were subjected to even harsher treatment.

The margrave listened patiently to this reckless disquisition of mine. When we were alone, he reacted to it in the following way:

"Do not be offended, sir, by my opinion of the principles, observations, and descriptions you have just given. I do not deny that the Nipuans are as perfect a people as human nature will permit, although I note that even amongst them there have been men who had to be stoned. I would say that your view of the Nipuans has tainted your opinion of Europeans much too greatly.

"If we require the highest degree of excellence in people, we will then not find anyone deemed worthy of our affection. And since friendship develops from similarities between people, he who seeks only truly excellent people displays exaggerated self-esteem, or seems to consider himself faultless. There are no Nipuans in Europe, but you must live among people. It is impossible to live and yet remain a stranger to the sweet bonds of friendship, so you will be forced to seek acquaintances. Do not make such quests laborious, and do not make them impossible. Grant a few imperfections in those you care to know well, and you will be happy, for then you will find friends.

"You observed a people who were kind, honest, and who love justice. You grew accustomed to them, and I am not surprised that you are now offended by what you behold, for I understand your position perfectly. But for that very same reason I make bold to warn you that to express your thoughts so openly as you have done to me is unwise. In certain circumstances you might suffer harm for so doing. There are few right-minded people in the world today. There are even fewer people who dare say what they really think. Consequently, though out of good-heartedness we do not conceal that which takes place in our world, because of good judgment we often do not reveal all that we think."

Chapter Eight

The captain's words caused the scales to fall from my eyes. I found it hard to understand how a mind so venerable could be compatible with that neat and shapely exterior. After thanking him for this salutary advice, I revealed my surprise at finding a true philosopher in the guise of a stylish young man.

"I do not so flatter myself," responded the margrave, "nor may I assume a title so grand. If, however, the first person who called himself a philosopher wanted to be a friend of wisdom, then I will be content to be a friend of philosophy. The philosopher strives for perfection but knows quite well that this is impossible to achieve. Those who employ the shaky foundations of their intellects to condemn what they cannot comprehend, while boldly maintaining that they comprehend everything, not only are unworthy of the title of philosopher but do not even deserve to be called thinking beings.

"Your wonderment at finding a young man, fashionably dressed, living comfortably, and yet not contemptuous of learning and philosophical reflections springs from a twofold prejudice: you attribute wisdom exclusively to old age, and you generalize excessively about people.

"Regarding the former, common sense and experience would lead one to conclude that the passions with all their force leave little room for sound and sensible judgment. In time the passions cool, and a field opens within the intellect for the exercise of judgment. Whether one governs a political body or simply one's family, one is forced to weigh and consider every step, for an error might offend or scandalize those subject to one's authority.

"With age people become more patient in investigating why things happen. They discuss things cautiously and exercise authority with restraint, for they are afraid of making mistakes. They persist in that which they feel certain of. Young people do not have these advantages. One need not conclude from this, however, that young people through diligence cannot acquire what older people possess thanks to age. A young person who is attentive and diligent is like the soil in those lands where the rays of the sun are so intense that one need not wait until autumn for the harvest.

"A generalization is nothing more than prejudice against shared character traits of nations. Your mistaken notions about me, as you yourself admit, are rooted in such prejudice. Since you were convinced that all Frenchmen are frivolous and fickle, you decided that my courteous treatment of you was superficial, if not duplicitous. I do not deny that our lively temperament encourages people to think in this way, but when such thoughts lead to extremes, the needless impetuosity of imagination is in need of tempering. The same animation that causes frivolity and flightiness in some, that same animation, I tell you, produces in others kindness, charity, candidness, and gentleness—qualities essential to civilized society.

"Politeness itself cannot be considered as one of the attributes essential to the soul, but politeness adorns all such attributes. Good deeds performed in a polite and kind manner have double value. We admire the severity of Cato's blunt virtue, but Socrates' gentle quality has a stronger effect on us. Cato commands respect, but we feel a certain repugnance toward him; Socrates inspires us to imitate and love him.

"Let us suppose that frivolity *is* a typical trait of the French character. Does it necessarily follow that all Frenchmen are flighty? If you will only take a closer look, you will find Frenchmen who are sedate, Germans who are sober, Spaniards who are humble, Muscovites who are sincere...The fact that your compatriots have no distinguishing trait of their own may or may not be a compliment."

Chapter Nine

Discussions such as these kept the voyage from becoming monotonous. We had favorable winds the whole time. The captain and his officers mitigated the unpleasantness usual in such a passage. The entire crew—one might say the small republic of the ship—were all affected by the kind and courteous manner of their commander. They were a model of harmony, each fulfilling his strenuous duties willingly.

After sailing several weeks, we passed the Canary Islands and entered the Straits of Gibraltar. I was filled with unspeakable joy at seeing European shores for the first time. The captain, sensitive to my feelings, joined in my pleasure. He gently intimated, however, that it is dangerous to fall prey to one's passions. He also observed that it can be harder to cope with happiness than unhappiness.

Eventually the captain asked what my plans were once we entered the port of Cádiz. I told him that I wanted simply to traverse Spain, spend a little time in France, and then return to my native land as quickly as possible. He offered to travel with me all the way to Paris, an offer that pleased me greatly. We had taken in some of the sights of Cádiz and had prepared everything for a trip on the Mediterranean to Marseilles when unexpected orders came, forcing a change in the margrave's plan. He was to convey the French consul then in Cádiz to Smyrna. Since the schedule for this trip was prescribed, he could not deviate from the itinerary to put me off in Marseilles.

Our leave-taking was extremely sad, especially since we found it hard to imagine that we would ever see one another again. So painful was it that I became almost a recluse for quite some time afterward. I knew no one, nor did I wish to meet anyone, even though I had ample opportunity to do so, living as I did in the city's foremost inn and taking my meals with people both from the area and abroad. Following the margrave's advice, I had sent all my drafts to Paris, where they were deposited with one of that city's most reputable bankers. Since I intended to settle my debts once I got to Paris, I invented the name of baron de Graumsdorff for myself, so that when word of the drafts' arrival became known, they would not be seized immediately by those to whom I was beholden.

Despite the wise admonitions of my friend, I was unable to restrain myself in conversation, inveighing against the wickedness of the nations of Europe and remarking how far removed they were from the virtuous simplicity of the Nipuans. My fellow boarders listened to these tirades more in amazement than with curiosity. The style of my clothing, fashioned to a degree along Nipuan lines, my way of greeting people with only a handshake and without removing my hat, and my overt sincerity were all things, I could tell, that my listeners found difficult to stomach. Moreover, when I spoke about the American natives and expatiated upon the cruelty of the people who had authority over them, they found my discussions repugnant.

Near the end of the third week of my sojourn in Cádiz, when I was returning one evening from a stroll, I suddenly found myself surrounded by soldiers at the gate. They forced me to give up my weapons, put me into a closed coach, and that night took me to a castle by the sea several miles from the city. There I was forced to sit in great discomfort for close to two months without uttering a word to anyone. The person who brought me food once a day looked like someone meant to guard a torture chamber. He met all my questions with silence. The sole word his lips emitted when he shut the doors each night was *adios*.

After a number of weeks, without a word spoken, I was removed and put in a carriage like the one I had come in, and following several days' travel, always at night, I arrived in a large city. I learned subsequently that I had been brought to Seville. I was put into a prison that was in better condition and more comfortable than the first one. The tall guard, old, shriveled, and sullen, did not even say *adios* to me. Fed poorly, usually with nothing more than an onion, lacking books, pen, paper, and inkpot, I was imprisoned for four months in a room with a narrow little window located high over my head. Had I been able to look out the window, I would have seen nothing. The wall was several ells thick, the window less than half an ell wide; the two iron bars of the grating barely permitted any light to creep in.

I had become convinced that I had been abandoned by the entire world and that I would have to spend the rest of my miserable days so confined, when, one day, without saying anything to me, the guard led me by the hand through a series of long, narrow, and dark passageways to a fairly large chamber that was lighter thanks to its single barred window. The walls of the chamber were bare and, like the vaulted ceiling, were blackened from what appeared to be the smoke and soot of torches or fires. In the middle stood a table covered with a black woolen cloth. At the head of the table was a leather armchair and around it wooden stools. On the table lay a crucifix.

Chapter Ten

Left alone in this horrible place, I waited with great trepidation to see what further turns my fate would take. All of a sudden, the doors opened with a bang, and in came a man wearing a black mantle who was even taller, even more shriveled, and paler than the guard. Behind him, also wearing black mantles, came four more men. Finally, there entered what must have been a scribe, with an inkpot hanging from his belt and papers in one hand.

The men took their places at the table. The one who had entered first sat down in the armchair and ordered me to draw near, kneel, lower my eyes, and raise one hand. I did as I was told. He then dictated a formal oath wherein I promised to respond truthfully, sincerely, accurately, fully, properly, and acceptably to any and all questions put to me. There were indeed many questions. First I had to state what country I had come from and what my name was. Since I desired to tell the whole truth, I admitted that the name I used was invented and that my real name was Wisdom. The scribe was not accustomed to foreign names. He had to write it down at least five times before he succeeded in recording it correctly, and then only after I had spelled it out for him. Additional questions were put to me touching on various aspects of my life. When I was asked about the conversations that had occurred at the dinner table of the inn in Cádiz, I noticed that the judges' interest increased and that more exact information was sought.

When it came time to make mention of Nipu, I described at length Nipuan customs, how the Nipuans governed themselves, and their way of life and manner of thinking. I praised their attributes and virtues and bemoaned the fact that I had fled so benevolent a society. At first the judges listened attentively, but halfway through the liveliest part of my account the solemn one abandoned his lofty and cheerless demeanor and began to laugh so loudly and so boisterously that he nearly fell out of his armchair. His comrades joined in his laughter. I was left dumbfounded.

One of the judges got up abruptly and, barely able to move because of all the laughing he had done, took hold of me by the arm and pushed me out of the room, closing the doors behind him. The incomprehensible laughter continued for more than half an hour. Then a bell rang in the chamber. My guard went in and, having been given, I surmised, instructions about what to do with me, led me downstairs to another chamber. There my arms were fettered, and in a short while a barber came, cut off my hair, and then shaved my head smooth.

At first I could not understand why all of this had happened. But in the wake of this last rite I began to realize that I had been judged insane. Before long a cart drew up, and after a little straw had been strewn in it, I was put in. This is how I got to the asylum. The overseer must have been told that I was not a harmful madman, for as soon as I arrived, the fetters were removed from my arms, and I was put in a recess more like a cage than a room. I feared I would be subjected to the initiation rite that I had heard was customarily administered to those entering such establishments—a greeting with lashes—but happily this was not the custom in Seville.[76]

For supper I was brought a little rice, a biscuit, and a small jug of water. Since I was accustomed to such dainties, I consumed everything with great relish. When night came, I lay down on a bed of straw. The new nature of my situation prevented me from sleeping for a long time. I had grown accustomed to misfortune, however, so I did not despair. Indeed, what I now experienced was a relief in comparison with my former situation. It was impossible, I told myself, for the overseers, supervisors, and physicians here not to realize that I was sane. And when they realized this, I would be freed.

Since my account of the Nipuans was the reason I had been declared insane, the Nipuans' maxims apparently here being the most important factor, I resolved firmly that, even though I might live differently from other people, I would nonetheless sound like other people when I talked. On Nipu I spoke and thought as a European and was judged a savage. In Europe I tried to comport myself in the Nipuan manner and was judged insane. Such thoughts brought the peculiarity of my fate into full relief; they also put me in a humorous frame of mind. In the end I found it hard to suppress a desire to laugh as I considered my shaven head and the place where the precepts of that fine mentor Xaoo had landed me.

The following day I was handed a container of feathers and a bundle of uncarded wool. The person who brought them let it be known through unmistakable gestures that laziness would not be tolerated. The work I performed that day and those following was easy to do. Compassionate people visited me and my fellow inmates. Their alms provided for our needs, and thanks to them the brutal treatment we sometimes suffered at the hands of the ill-mannered keepers was mitigated.

The chaplain of the asylum, a noble-minded old gentleman, often consoled me in my troubles, but I was never able to persuade him that I was not insane. He would talk to me about divine disposition, about how one who has lost his reason because of divine disposition ought to be resigned to his fate, how my lack of faith was the most important proof of my insanity, and how the verdict of my investigators was more conclusive than any evidence I might give to the contrary. He spoke from the heart and was so convincing that he could have persuaded anyone to question his own sanity. When I realized that my arguments did not convince him in any way, shape, or form, I asked that a physician be summoned to examine all the evidence and pass judgment on my condition.

A man advanced in age appeared. He wore an enormous wig, an enormous hat, an enormous coat, and on his nose were enormous spectacles. He took my hand, measured my pulse, peered twice into my eyes, shook his head several times, and then closed his eyes for a minute or two. Turning to the overseer, he said in a grave tone of voice: "Insane!" and left the room. The physician's judgment made me so angry that I was ready to run after him so that I could punish him. But I was afraid that if I did this I would merely lend greater credence to his opinion.

I kept my peace for several weeks after this incident. One day I noticed that foreigners had come to inspect our hospital. The reader can easily imagine the joy I felt when I caught sight of the margrave de Vennes among them. I fell to his feet. At first he stood stock-still, then raised me from the ground. When he heard about my adventures, he immediately rushed to those in high authority. He returned in two hours with a release order and conducted me thence to his lodgings.

Chapter Eleven

Since I had experienced such odd turns of fate so many times, I found it hard to believe that what I saw and felt was real. My friend's humane act, his gentle bearing, and feelings of deep affection made me feel I could not have been more fortunate in choice of company. We quickly abandoned Seville, the capital of Andalusia. The country around this city is most beautiful. Would that the memory of my unhappy adventures there had not made it so hateful. It was not long before we arrived in Madrid. We stayed there only a short time before setting out for France. When we passed through the Pyrenees, the margrave welcomed me to his native land. I will not waste time describing the countryside and cities; that is the responsibility of geographers. After traversing much of France, we reached Paris. I revealed my true name and appeased those to whom both M. Fickiewicz and I owed money. The capital remaining after my assets were sold and the drafts all redeemed—nearly a million ducats—I dispatched to Poland through bankers.

Although I was eager to visit my native land, I stayed several weeks in Paris, honored to be able to share the margrave's company. I became acquainted with many worthy and highly respected people who frequented his home, and it was this experience more than anything else that helped me overcome my tendency to generalize about nations. There in the middle of Paris I found sages who were not proud, rich men who were not haughty, noblemen who were accessible, God-fearing people who were neither bigoted nor spiteful, and knights who did not boast.

I was so fascinated by the pleasant company of these people that I was on the verge of deciding to settle permanently in Paris. I revealed my thoughts to the margrave and requested his counsel before making arrangements to do so. In response he said the following:

"If, as I believe, one motive for wanting to live in Paris is to continue our association, I am both flattered and grateful. If I were to search deep in my heart, I am certain I could come up with additional reasons why you should stay here with us. But in cases of genuine friendship, it is not unusual to sacrifice one's personal pleasure, especially when it is a matter of fulfilling basic responsibilities. You owe your fatherland your presence there as a citizen. To those of honest mind the word *citizen* is not without meaning. It is a calling that entails responsibilities. Indeed, the first and most all-embracing of these is that one should be of the greatest possible use to his native land. To defend one's country courageously or to administer it well are not the only ways to serve one's country: there are other ways of fulfilling this duty, and no citizen is exempt from doing so. You were born into the gentry. Your talents, which have been refined by experience, qualify you for this service. It may well happen, in fact it is almost certain to, that you will not be properly rewarded for serving your country. Rewards are often denied to those who merit them. You will, however, be able to take consolation in the knowledge that you have acted properly, and this will serve as your reward. I speak to you thus with *your* welfare in mind, not my own. Your absence will be painful, but my pain will be eased when I recall that virtuous friend and useful citizen of Poland named Wisdom."

There was nothing I could say in response to these remarks. In a few days, having put my affairs in order, I sorrowfully took leave of the margrave.

Chapter Twelve

The account of my trip from Paris to Warsaw would not be of interest to the reader. Not a single adventure of any note transpired. The days were beautiful, the roads smooth. I arrived in Warsaw on May 14, precisely at noon. I was introduced to the court, the noblemen receiving me graciously, the ladies warmly. Everyone eyed me curiously, eager to learn all the details of my adventures, since word of such, complete with the usual embellishments, had long preceded me.

I was much in demand because I was unusual. And the fact that people knew that I had acquired riches in no way detracted from my desirability. I tried to avoid being the object of this irksome curiosity. Fortunately, an Englishman soon arrived who immediately became an object of interest. My fifteen days of questioning were over, and I could breathe freely again. Because of the powerful backing I enjoyed, I was able to satisfy my creditors. I reclaimed

Szumin and the small villages I had inherited and entrusted the rest of my capital to a wealthy, but serious and honest, gentleman so that he would invest it and pay me the income that accrued.

I then made my way to the law courts. There I was completely victorious in the case with my old plenipotentiary, who by legal subterfuge had tried to retain possession of several of my villages. I was fortunate to be in a court where name days were not celebrated, where the reverend president did not have a nephew, and where the deputies did not demand to take other people's calashes home, never to return them.

On my first visit to Szumin, now mine once again, all those places associated with my younger days gave me indescribable pleasure. The grove and brook reminded me of Julie, the pond of the mishap she witnessed, and the tiny rooms forming the annex of the education in feeling that M. Damon had given me. The old servants wept upon seeing me; the serfs let out a joyous cry to proclaim the return of the true heir. I was happy to settle in the country, having had too much city noise, too many disturbances, and too much wandering. In the course of ten years I had been a courtier in Warsaw, a gallant in Paris, a tiller of the soil on Nipu, a slave in Potosí, and a madman in Seville. Now in Szumin I became a philosopher.[77]

First, so that the happiness of the Nipuans and the sacred precepts of my teacher Xaoo would always remain fresh in my mind, I ordered that a house just like the one in which Xaoo lived be constructed not far from my residence. An orchard, brook, pond, and field, all on the same scale as those on Nipu, were laid out to give me the illusion of that pleasant life I had known. No matter how many times I go there, the memory of Nipu's salutary customs and principles always provides me with food for thought. Thanks to my visits there I am what I am. My serfs are satisfied with me, my neighbors do not quarrel with me, and I enjoy peace within my home and harmony without.

I deemed the happiness of my serfs uppermost in the management of my property. My neighbors were scandalized by this. They said it would do me no good to carry out such measures. Some pitied me, others laughed at my naïveté. Now they see that my farmland is better cultivated than theirs, no rents are in arrears, my barns are twice as full, and my peasants are well dressed and sit in the front pews of the parish church.

I had led a most happy and carefree life for nearly a year, when I received a letter from a minister in Warsaw inviting me to launch a career of great promise by agreeing to represent my province in the next Diet. Neither ambition nor cupidity lured me. I gave only as much value to the promise as I thought it worth, having experienced earlier the moral value of the coin of the court. I recalled, however, my last conversation with the margrave and decided to attend the sessions of our provincial dietine. Heeding the advice of my neighbors, I first paid visits to all the local officials. Although it was my firm intention to remain temperate, despite heroic efforts I was nonetheless forced to get drunk several times.

In the capital city proper, I tried to become a representative to the Diet by walking the straight and narrow path. My neighbors called me uncivilized for bringing only one cook with me. When they found out that I had a mere two barrels of wine, the lord chamberlain himself stated bluntly that there was little hope of my being chosen. Consequently, I brought as quickly as I could several kegs of good wine from the nearest cloister. Neighbors lent me cooks. And since money was abundant, everything was done quickly and turned out well.

Quite a few of us competed as candidates. The gentry could choose only two delegates. On the eve of the day the dietine was to assemble, the pantler who was assigned to me announced that I would prevail over my strongest competitor only if I distributed large sums of money to the nobles. The baseness, not the avarice, of this proposal caused me to heave a sigh and recall that fortunate isle where citizens' intelligence and the public will were not for sale.

The din in the church where the dietine had assembled increased, and a fight broke out near the narthex even before the opening speech had ended. We dashed between drunkards, and when we attempted to find out why our opponents had grown so impassioned, we could ascertain only that it probably was due to the fact that they had eaten breakfast at the house of the sword-bearer. I was presented as a candidate. Quite unexpectedly, my old plenipotentiary emerged from behind the high altar and read the verdict I had received in abstentia.[78] Zealous friends of mine wanted to hack him to pieces. Fortunately, he escaped into the sacristy and closed the door behind him. We then proceeded to negotiate with him through a peephole. He withdrew his claims, and I was made a delegate. I invited everyone to my place for a grand feast. There, in accordance with ancient custom, everyone got drunk in the name of love and harmony.

Chapter Thirteen

The following day, while I was still abed sleeping off the previous day's inebriation, the chamberlain sent a messenger requesting my presence. At his quarters I found several high officials speaking in animated fashion. I learned from a colleague of mine who was also present that they were composing instructions for us to follow during the sessions of the Diet.[79] I found it very surprising that when it was a matter of choosing representatives, everyone took part, but when it came to the more important matter of formulating how these representatives were to act, only a few officials and members of the gentry participated. When I was informed, however, that this had long been the custom, I kept my peace.

The time came to read the particulars of our instructions. Not a single one had to do with the commonweal. Instead, there were recommendations for persons to fill senatorial seats and ministerial posts. A large number of people was recommended for dispensations of *panis bene merentium* by His Gracious Majesty.[80] A request for money to repair the Lublin and Piotr city halls was then added.[81] When the reading was finished, the nestor from our region, His Honor the District Judge, took the floor. He expostulated on the need to keep the commonweal first and foremost, citing the text *salus publica suprema lex esto*.[82] Then, in his capacity as district judge, he entreated us to make *pro primo et principali obiecto*[83] instruction of the honorable delegates chosen from among their peers in the matter of the Neapolitan sums and the opening of the mines in Olkusz.[84] Everyone agreed, and this point was appended to our instructions. Added also was the approval of several endowments[85] and the canonization of two saints recently beatified.

Before it came time to sign the instructions, I took the floor. After I had expressed my gratitude to my peers for choosing me, I warned them not to take what I was about to say regarding the instructions as a sign of impudence.

"What provides greater incentive to fulfill promises and meet obligations more than any oath is a sense of dignity. The newly composed instructions that your lordships and these peers of mine have vested in us will serve as a set of guiding principles for us to follow in the forthcoming Diet. Since I understand them as such, I trust that you will not be angry at us, or at me in particular, for having the courage to speak out and present you with arguments concerning the instructions, arguments designed to safeguard those fragile items known as honor and virtue.

"The person designated to represent the people of our entire province is an important public official. His actions, therefore, should be consistent with his obligations to those he represents. I believe that a person in the public eye should occupy himself exclusively with matters in the public's interest. If such a person deigns to consider lesser matters, he does so because he wants in one way or another to subvert the goal of the public good for the sake of his own private interests. Our fatherland has many needs, but none of them were mentioned in the instructions just read. By adding the statement 'We leave *caetera activitati* to the honorable delegates,' we are not really providing protection for those who boldly offer proposals good for our country but that your lordships may not find to your liking.[86] This I say sorrowfully, but with firm conviction, for I have often seen the best intentions go astray and zeal for the public good penalized because it conflicted with the interests of citizens who only profited at the public's expense.

"Thus, when we compose instructions, let us consider the needs of our fatherland. Let us propose ways to restore it to health and succor it, and let nominations to office, war reparations, and canonizations wait for the nonce. The phrase '*etiam sub discrimine* the Diet' seems to me not only superfluous but also insulting to those whom you gentlemen send out *non ad destructionem, sed ad aedi-*

ficationem.[87] I will not launch into a discussion of whether it is appropriate or even lawful to break off Diets. Permit me to observe that I see such *abusum,* such baseness and wickedness in the disruption of public debate, that I think that a person who does so, while he has the honor of representing your lordships, greatly debases himself. I see only two items concerned with the public good in our instructions: recovery of the Neapolitan sums and reopening the Olkuszian mines. I understand that several dozen matters left unresolved by previous Diets shall be tabled for consideration by the next one. I do not know whether this embellishes, improves, or spoils these important matters. I will not fail to mention this at the proper time. As for those noblemen recommended for special compensation, I ask each of you to evaluate his service for me. If I can demonstrate your worthy deeds to the general assembly of the *res publica,* I can be bold in my demand for recompense."

I stopped speaking. A short silence ensued, which ended when the chamberlain, who was presiding, expressed his approval of the *zelum boni publici* in one who, although new to public life, demonstrated this attribute so well.[88] After many and sundry digressions, he quoted Philip, king of Macedonia. He then proceeded to eulogize old Polish virtues and jauntily concluded: "That's the way it is, and it cannot be otherwise, noble peers and brethren. Things were better for our forebears, when there was no thought of traveling abroad. While we were content with that which the Good Lord by His Grace has given us, both cow shed and barn were full. Now everything is done with fashion in mind, like the French, or the Germans, or the devil knows like what. Calves are now cleverer than oxen. Let them say what they want, but an ox is still an ox, a calf no more than a calf."

There was laughter. I wanted to take the floor a second time, but my good friend the purse-bearer whispered in my ear that I would gain nothing, offend everyone, that in the vestibule the gentry were already in turmoil, saying that I was a heretic. I was alarmed by this news, and so, like it or not, I laughed with the others and admired the subtle wit of the chamberlain who so magnificently understood and defended the national honor and the virtues of our forefathers.

Chapter Fourteen

After the successful completion of the dietine, I rested for a time at home, then journeyed to the Diet in Warsaw, filled with patriotic principles and ardor for the public good. I had composed a speech on the Neapolitan sums and, had time permitted, I would have made a special trip to Olkusz to gain more detailed information about the mines and the merits of reopening them.

I found lodgings in a suburb of the capital. Shortly after I arrived, a distinguished gentleman residing in the city paid me a visit. He congratulated me in the name of the fatherland for the honor of being chosen a representative. He then looked all around and, although we were alone in the room, took me by the hand and with a knowing look led me to an alcove where he left me so that he could busily inspect every nook and cranny in the place. After doing this he closed and locked the doors to the entrance hall. I decided he must be preparing to ask me for a loan. He returned rubbing his hands. Getting very close to me and standing on tiptoe he whispered in my ear: "Dear friend! I give you my word that I will not betray you, but please be so good as to tell me what party you belong to."

I returned to the center of the room despite his efforts to prevent me from doing so. Once we were seated, I stated that I could not answer his question because I did not know what the word *party* meant nor how it was connected with my position and duties. "A good citizen," I went on, "does not debase his own intelligence by surrendering to someone else's opinion. The word *party* would appear to mean leaders on the one hand and partisans on the other. In practical terms, however, it means imperious tyrants and hired lackeys. In a country called a republic, where by definition freedom and equality should prevail, how a state of affairs so sordid and so vile finds countenance is to me incomprehensible. Furthermore, he who gives orders to an equal is unduly impudent, and he who obeys an equal for profit or favor is vile indeed. Let the poorest citizen instruct me about my duties, and I will gladly heed his opinion. A yearly 'contribution' or a gift of a village as an annuity is, however, not a good way to salve my conscience. I thus find it surprising that you pose this question. I imagine you do this in jest..."

"One can tell that you have come from a very distant island" was his reply, and bowing, he left.

The following day I was invited to dinner at the home of a dignitary. Also there was our voivode, who greeted me and said in a low voice: "I do not question your opinions and am honored to have your friendship. I am ready to serve you and ask that you tell me what would please you."

I dismissed his declaration of esteem for me with a bow. At this point the dignitary entered and recommended in the name of the court that the marshal of the Diet favor one of the delegates.

For supper I was invited to the home of a senator. Because he had not been given a recently vacated sinecure, the senator bemoaned the fact that Poland was being ruined by court intrigues. He recommended that his own nephew, who at the tender age of five had been made a lieutenant colonel, be shown special favor by the marshal. The nephew, now nineteen years old, was anxious to have a regiment of his own. Solicitations came from all sides, but I did not compromise my honor, nor did I make promises.

The opening day of the Diet arrived. We entered the chamber; with the usual ceremonies the marshal of the previous Diet began the session amid great commotion and a deafening roar.

After two days we tired of waiting for a new marshal to be elected. On the third day a decree was issued that adjourned the Diet. Six months' effort and expense by the public ended with a dismal oration by the former marshal, who mournfully lamented the unhappy fate of the fatherland.

I wanted to acquaint myself with the way life was conducted at court and afford myself an opportunity for an official appointment, so I remained in Warsaw amid a throng of people hungering for the same. For several months I attempted to gain office in various ways, but when I began to think about what I might gain and how, I changed my mind. Everyone repeated what the first gentleman who visited me in Warsaw had said, namely, that I must have come from a very distant island.

Chapter Fifteen

I did not succeed in Warsaw, but this did not make me angry at Warsaw or the human race. Everyone has his own approach to things. Mine was not in agreement with Warsaw's, so I went to Szumin to think.

He who goes to the country solely to think should prepare himself to feel boredom and disgust. Those who depict country life as bliss do so for the most part surrounded by urban distractions. They imagine the study in which they isolate themselves to be an exquisite grove, a beautiful valley. At the command of poets, winding brooks begin to flow, foamy streams cascade down over cliffs, and the twittering of little birds echoes through the woods and amid the cliffs. But just try to make these vivid phrases agree with your own experience, and you will find that you have asked for a lot and must settle for a little. Nature is not lavish in the way it provides its charms. Those sights produced by our nimble imagination present, to be sure, a pleasant and charming picture, but a picture quite different from the one originally conceived. One can presumably find other sources for poetic inspiration in romances or fables.

Country life is pleasant because it makes one want to engage in farming, that honorable, year-round occupation. The farmer's desire for profit, combined with the natural and ever-changing activities he enjoys, prevents melancholy from developing, that melancholy that is habitually experienced when one is exhausted by the distractions of the city.

Once settled again at home, I felt as if I had returned to my island. I was the first landowner in the entire region, it seemed, who did not doubt that his serfs were human. And so I set myself the task of making their lot more bearable. That small body of right-minded people will attest to the heartfelt joy one experiences in being able to bring happiness to one's fellow men. It was said that I had come back from a very distant island; that was the judgment that had blocked the way to my advancement. If *return* means that virtue and happiness are incompatible, then I recommend that my countrymen travel to distant islands. Even if they happen to pass by Paris and London in the course of their journey, the fatherland will not suffer.

I trust that the reader will forgive me for this short digression. As one battered by various adventures, it is only natural that I should feel the sweet pleasure of a good rest more strongly than others. And while resting, I began to think about marriage and about giving my children a good education and in that way being of service to the nation.

Not far from my village lived an aristocrat who, though of ancient and virtuous lineage, was impecunious. Portraits of his forebears, some holding maces, others marshals' staffs, crosiers, seals, spiked clubs, and the like, filled a hall in his palace. Since I was much better off than the master of this house, I went there assuming that my bid for the hand of his daughter, who seemed well educated, would be joyfully accepted. I made my intentions known through a close friend. Such "impudence" was not to that lord's taste. Over supper he launched into a speech on the prerogatives that came with a celebrated and great family name and on the pettiness of parents who for the sake of trivial material gain are willing to unite aristocracy with common gentry. Her ladyship looked at me with an eye full of scorn as well as majesty. The rest I could surmise, and so the next day precisely at dawn I rode away without so much as a farewell, sorely distressed that my coat of arms lacked crown and mantle.

In the area there was another lady, not from a family so grand, but whose father, the best-known participant in the Lvovian Exchanges, despised all the vanitites of this world except for ducats of pure gold and old talers. At the aristocrat's house we had eaten pheasant served on bone china. The associate judge served me borscht, roast pork, cabbage stew, and beets on silver dishes with, I noticed, his lordship's coat of arms with crown and mantle engraved on them. Without discussing my personal qualities at all, the associate judge immediately proposed that I formally endow my future spouse with an amount equal to one half of the dowry and arrange to have the remainder of my fortune made into an annuity for her. The proposition was repugnant to me, but no less repugnant than the lady herself, who was all puffed up by the size of her dowry and lacked good qualities.

In time, at a church fair, I made the acquaintance of a very beautiful, but poor, young noblewoman. I would have declared my intentions to her parents had I not noticed one day when she was absent a note penned in her hand on a little table addressed to a local court official of lower rank announcing her forthcoming marriage. In the note she regretted that virtue and good character rarely accompany wealth and in closing declared that, although she would live a comfortable life with her husband, her heart would always belong to dear Antonio. Not happy with the prospect of sharing this young lady with Antonio, I chose not to appear in that house again.

Chapter Sixteen

These disappointing efforts at courtship dampened my resolve to marry, and I retreated once again to my home. So as not to be regarded for the third time as an eccentric, however, I chose several good and reasonable neighbors and visited them now and then. And when they returned my visits, I received them warmly. Otherwise I devoted my time to agriculture, building, my orchard, and books. I led this worthwhile life for nearly a year and in the course of doing so rebuilt the old walls of our fine ancestral castle, turning it into a comfortable and attractive home. In the midst of all this an uncle died and left me property in Lithuania, occasioning a trip there.

I went to Lithuania at the worst time of year for travel—spring. One day in a marshy area, a bridge broke under my carriage. I sent to the nearest village for horses. Finding there none for hire, my servants went to a nearby manor. The lady who owned the estate obliged them. After learning what my name was, where I resided, the reason for my trip, and many other details, she immediately sent her personal carriage and enough horses to draw my carriage and the other vehicles I had brought along. The courtier who brought the carriage paid me compliments in his mistress's name, saying that, although her ladyship was sorry to learn of my mishap, she congratulated herself for having an opportunity to receive me as a guest in her home.

I got into the carriage willingly, curious to meet this polite young widow (I was told that she had been widowed for three years). I was driven to a beautiful palace, a palace with apartments that were as comfortable as they were grand. The lady who received me was not only young and polite but also beautiful, and she showed me every kindness. I thanked her for being so obliging. In the palace I found a great many guests. A lavish table was maintained, and guests were entertained in a way difficult to equal in the finest cities. The quarters assigned to me were comfortable and attractive, and exhausted by the vicissitudes of my journey, I rested well in them. The next day after dinner, when I was ready to bid my hostess farewell, she said playfully that if I would not stay several more days, she would order the bridges and dams in the villages on her land through which I would pass to be weakened like the one I had encountered on her neighbor's estate. Captivated by her eyes and by her affability, I readily consented.

One day after dinner, when the guests had gone their respective ways and we were alone, she said: "Sir, you have satisfied my curiosity with your descriptions of your adventures abroad. Please be so good as to tell me now about your adventures in your own country starting from the time you were very young."

"They are not remarkable," I said. "I cannot, however, refuse to obey such a gentle command, and so I will try to give you a faithful account of them."

I began to relate the story of my parents, M. Damon and his education of feeling, and my reading of romances. In connection with the last I made reference to the incident in the copse where I had first declared my love to Julie, my mother's ward. Pleasant memories made me wax eloquent, and with tears in my eyes I added that we had had a painful leave-taking after which Julie had been lost to my sight though not to my heart.

"I have an abundance of everything now," I continued, "but I am saddened by the fact that she cannot share my prosperity. I have not been able to learn where she now resides. At the convent where she was sent I was told only than an aunt had taken her in.

To date no one has told me the name of this aunt or her where-abouts. The only thing that soothes me in my grief is the ring Julie gave me, which I keep with me at all times; when we took leave of one another, I gave her one too."

I had scarcely finished when she gave me her hand. A veil fell from my eyes: I saw the ring I had given Julie and realized it was she. I fell to her feet, and I apologized that my eyes and heart had not been in harmony. It is easy to forgive the one who loves you. As the reader can imagine, exuberant expressions of joy, wonder, and curiosity interrupted our conversation again and again. Amid this tumult of lively and passionate feelings I could hear my happiness being pronounced...someone loved me.

Chapter Seventeen

It is customary for romances to end with a set of extraordinary adventures that bring the characters together in one spot so that they may recognize or find one another. My spontaneous recognition of Julie and our reacquaintance after all my many adventures and ten years of separation bear a resemblance to the style of romances, except for the fact that the two of us met in Julie's own home. We did not search for one another over land and sea.

As you may well surmise, I asked Julie how she came to be what she was. Had I wished to adhere to the style of romances, I would have made a fourth book out of Julie's story. I would have related in separate chapters, for example, how Julie had been locked up in a cloister, how she had greatly mourned the loss of the man who loved her, how once while walking in the cloister's garden with companions she had been forcibly abducted by unknown persons, how she had been seized by other unknown persons in some faraway wilderness, how these persons had taken her to dreadful dungeons and caves, how she had had to endure much in these dreadful dungeons and caves and had escaped from them at great personal risk, how after a lengthy peregrination she had come upon a male or female anchorite, how this anchorite (who would have had to have been very old) nourished her for a time solely on roots, how an important gentleman who was out hunting had happened upon the anchorite's dwelling and was smitten at the mere sight of her, how that important gentleman had disguised himself and visited her a second time, persuading her to abandon the life of an ascetic, how she had let herself be so persuaded and had become his wife, how this husband had fallen ill and had died and was buried, and how she had inherited his entire estate, and so forth and so on.

Julie's experiences were not so extraordinary as that: an aunt took her out of the convent and brought her to Lithuania. A wealthy widower made her acquaintance, liked her, wished to marry her, and did so. Having no close relatives of his own, he bequeathed his fortune to her and in a year's time died himself.

Those truly in love do not require refined declarations of affection for one another. To offer my unending service—which was not refused—and thereby win the hand and heart of my beloved Julie took no more than a week. We have lived together happily ever since and are already grandparents. Julie remains the same in my eyes as she was then, years ago in the copse...

You have caught me unawares, my beloved wife, Julie! I want to tell the whole world how you sweeten my existence. May young people learn from our happiness that love founded on mutual respect never dies and that in a happy marriage the wrinkles of a kindhearted wife are far more agreeable than the fickle caresses of unfaithful mistresses.

The End of the Third and Final Book of Wisdom's Adventures

Berlin, February 26, 1775

Notes

1. "Can resentment so fierce dwell in a heavenly breast?" Virgil, *Aeneid* 1.11, trans. H. Rushton Fairclough, Loeb Classical Library (Cambridge: Harvard University Press, 1924).

2. Zoilus, a fourth-century B.C. rhetorician and critic, infamous for his severe criticism of Homer's poetry.

3. Nicolas Boileau-Despréaux (1636–1711), French literary critic and poet, the spokesman for neoclassicism in seventeenth-century French letters. In his Satire 9 (*A son spirit*) Boileau makes fun of the posturings of writers. (Annotations are taken principally from the seventh edition of *Mikołaja Doświadczyńskiego przypadki* [Wrocław, 1975], edited by Mieczysław Klimowicz, hereafter "MK.")

4. Talks given at school functions published with dedications to important persons (MK).

5. Paprocki's genealogy appeared in 1584, Okolski's in 1641–45, and Niesiecki's in 1728–43 (MK).

6. The legendary founders of the Czech and Polish nations.

7. Traditionally, the sons of the gentry were sent to grammar schools run by monks, where the poor and rich mingled. Only the wealthiest magnates engaged private teachers for their children (MK).

8. Examples of devotional literature very popular in the eighteenth century, but now almost entirely forgotten (MK).

9. Cyrus, Clélie, Alcander, Mandane, Dorine, and Cléomire are heroes and heroines of the romances *Artamène ou le Grand Cyrus* (1649–53) and *Clélie, histoire romaine* (1654–60), from the pen of French writer Madeleine de Scudéry, the most popular author of "volumes of love and morals" (MK).

10. Hippolyte and Julie are the protagonists of a French romance popular in the eighteenth century by writer Madame d'Aulnoy, *Hippolyte, comte de Douglas* (1690) (MK).

11. Flush (*tryszak,* or *tryseta*), matrimony, piquet, and reversi were popular gambling card games of the time. Cardinal de Fleury (André Hecule de Fleury [1653–1743] was a powerful adviser of Louis XV (MK, citing *Wokół*

'Doświadczyńskiego.' Antologia romansu i powieści [*'Mr. Nicholas Wisdom,'
Anthology of Romance and Novel*], (Warsaw, 1969), edited by Jerzy Jackl,
hereafter "JJ").

12. A romance by the Italian poet Giovanni Amrogio Marini, entitled
Calloandro sconosciuto (1640).

13. Coach attendants, normally of magnates, clad in the traditional military
uniform of Hungary.

14. Lovebirds are monogamous. Folk tradition has it that after the male's
death, the female remains faithful to him, lamenting him plaintively (MK).

15. Card games popular in the eighteenth century at which one stood to
lose considerable sums of money.

16. Gatherings of nobles held annually during the fairs at Dubno, in
Volhynia, and later at Lvov for business and social purposes. Various cheats,
cardsharpers, and forgers were drawn to the exchanges (MK).

17. In eighteenth-century Poland, "deputies" were judges of a high court
elected by the populace of districts and provinces.

18. *Volanti sigillo*, "unsealed."

19. *Sitiens justitiam*, "craving justice."

20. The crown court for the Malopolska, Ruthenia, and Podlasie regions of
Poland was at this time in Lublin. As the court's president in 1765, Krasicki
became well acquainted with the ways in which it operated (MK).

21. The court of Wielkopolska and Mazowsze was located in Piotrków.

22. Polish dignitaries considered it important to have flunkies of various
nationalities. If such were not to be had, serfs who had been made house
servants were given "borrowed" names and attire.

23. The crown's court deliberated in Piotrków from September 1 until the
first Sunday of Lent, then moved to Lublin for a term running from the second
Sunday after Easter until December 19. Thus "His Honor, John" celebrated
his name day in Piotrków on December 27, on St. John the Evangelist's Day,
and again in Lublin on April 24, on the feast of St. John the Baptist (MK).

24. A caste of legal personnel, some serving as defense counsels in cases
brought by individuals, others scribes who transcribed among other things
orders, grievances, summonses, and other legal writs that had been entered into
the public record.

25. "A legal term meaning a single part of a lawsuit," writes Krasicki,
"argued in court in such a way as to enable one side to win one category, the
other side another, so that both sides can claim victory." *Zbiór potrzebniejszych
wiadomości* (*A Collection of Essential Information*, 1781), in *Dzieła* (*Collected
Works*) (Warsaw, 1830), *Dopełnienia (Supplement)* 2:75 (JJ and MK).

26. The Book of Judgments contained detailed transcriptions of court
resolutions. Its records served as the basis for later judicial decisions (MK).

27. Lists of records or short digests of them (MK).

28. A traditional coat with split sleeves worn by Polish noblemen.

29. A long gown, the Polish nobleman's traditional costume.

30. Courts had two chairmen: a president, delegated by the clergy, and a marshal, chosen from the lay deputies (MK).

31. Cases brought to court were divided into eight categories and entered at eight corresponding registries. Cases involving divestiture of property or improper seizure of property were introduced at the Expulsionum Registry (MK).

32. Formulation of an issue from the point of view of legal requirements. In this instance the issue is whether Wisdom in fact had the right to the property seized by means of a foray (JJ).

33. At the Provincial Registry cases transmitted from lower courts and appeals from municipal and district courts were introduced (MK).

34. Here prefects ruled on cases involving largely robbery and raids (MK).

35. "Care was taken first to grant the more powerful litigants dismissals *per non sunt,* i.e., as if none of the individuals whose cases were called up or their plenipotentiaries were present. In this way the marshal, or whoever was serving in his stead, accommodated the most important petitioners. No one cared about the lesser ones. The marshal would order case after case to be called up and, paying no attention to the utterances of those declaring themselves present, would announce and write on the docket '*non sunt, non sunt,*' until he reached the case he had promised to let come up for trial." Jędzej Kitowicz, *Opis obyczajów za panowania August III (A Description of Customs during the Reign of August III),* 3d ed. (Wrocław, 1970), 203 (MK).

36. A legal document that, entered into the city or district registers in full detail, had the effect of law (MK).

37. *Łopata* means "spade."

38. The record of an official inspection of land in litigation (MK).

39. *Praedium militare alias,* "the prince's demense or, in other words."

40. *Abrenunciarunt,* "renounced their inheritances."

41. Cases entered on the Tapping Registry were those involving crimes committed by litigants or against the person of a deputy. When delivering a summons to those accused of such transgressions, the court usher tapped the accused on the shoulder (JJ).

42. A regulation designating set days of the week on which cases from particular dockets had to be considered (MK).

43. Kitowicz writes (p. 203) the following about this abuse: "When the marshal was not on the same side as they, the deputies committed to excluding a case would suddenly cut off the session by feigning illness, leaving the

courtroom suddenly, or by resting in bed several days at their lodgings until the time passed during which the register concerned was to be acted on" (MK).

44. Initial formalities in a trial (MK).

45. *Inducant negotium,* "let the trial begin."

46. *Pro temerario recessu et extenuatione temporis,* "for willful withdrawal and impeding justice."

47. "The winning cause pleased the gods, but the losing cause pleased Cato." Lucan, *Pharsalia,* 1.128, trans. Robert Graves (Baltimore: Penguin, 1957).

48. *Ingens gloria Dardanorum,* "great is the pride of the Dardani."

49. "The wreckage would immolate him unafraid." Horace, *Odes* 3.3.8, trans. W. G. Shepherd (Harmondsworth, Eng.: Penguin, 1983).

50. Stanisław Józef Duńczewski (1701–66), a Jesuit, astronomer, and author of popular almanacs (JJ).

51. The amount accruing from penalties and charges for conducting a trial paid by the losing side. The money was divided among the deputies (MK).

52. Verdict by default that, in contrast to the usual verdict, entailed forfeiture of protections under common law (MK).

53. On the condition that the money for the fine will be returned once it has been exacted from the one on whom judgment was passed (MK).

54. While president of the Małopolska court, Krasicki tried to bring about improvement in the training of judges and members of the bar, whom he regarded as lawyers only in name (MK).

55. A minor court official in the city hall who received testimony from parties and then entered it into the record. Among the various types of testimony recorded were formal complaints needed to start a trial (MK).

56. An old Polish legal formula, pertaining to the purchase and sale of real estate, made up of "macaronic" Latin: "boris" derives from the Polish *bór,* or "woods"; "gais" from *gaj,* or "grove"; and "graniciebus" from *granica,* or "boundary."

57. *Formalitatem,* "regulations."

58. A dependent was a trainee at a court or with a lawyer. An agent was an apprentice to the *palestra,* a secretary to a lawyer (MK).

59. *Faciamus experimentum in anima vili,* "let's perform an experiment on the wretched creature."

60. *De noviter repertis documentis,* "on the basis of records newly discovered."

61. Usurious interest for this time (MK).

62. A small city in Kielce province where in the eighteenth century haberdashers' shops produced piping, belts, and fringes for decorating clothing (MK).

63. Present-day Bielsko.

64. A city in Moravia, site of an Austrian citadel (MK).

65. A gibe at the Austrians for not erecting a monument to Polish king Jan Sobieski, who had saved Vienna from the Turks in 1683.

66. One of the seven electors of the German Reich who gathered in Frankfurt to choose the kaiser (MK).

67. A muff made of white bear cub fur, in eighteenth-century Poland used by both men and women (MK).

68. A prison in Paris where insolvent debtors, among others, were incarcerated (MK).

69. In the eighteenth century the greater part of Flanders was under the rule of the Hapsburgs (MK).

70. In 1747 the Republic party of the States-General lost power in Holland, and William IV of Orange became hereditary stadtholder.

71. Here Krasicki's target is astrology, which at this time in Poland was still considered one of the branches of physics (MK).

72. The views expressed here echo physiocratic economic theories, which propound that the earth is the source of all wealth and that consequently agriculture is the basis of a nation's economy and the tillers of the soil its most important class of people. Physiocratic theories developed in mid–eighteenth-century France and found numerous adherents in Poland (MK).

73. The fourfold division of education is similar to that found in Rousseau's *Émile*. Krasicki places more emphasis on the civic aspect of education than does Rousseau. Also noteworthy in the Nipuan educational program is the absence of religion (JJ).

74. The phrase appears in Homer, *Odyssey* 1.57, and Ovid, *Ex Ponto* 1.3.35.

75. Krasicki's notion that the Nipuan utopia perpetuated the way of life of ancient Peruvian Indians, that is, of the Incas, was based on the belief, shared by many thinkers of the Enlightenment, that the ancient American Indians were "children of nature" and had not been corrupted by the evil and the pride inherent in civilized societies. The life of the ancient Indians was idealized in the writings of the time, such as Jean-François Marmontel's *Les Incas* or Madame de Graffigny's *Lettres d'une Péruvienne*. Doubtless the chronicles of Garcilaso de la Vega, *Primera parte de los commentarios reales de los Incas* (Lisbon, 1609), as well as *Historia general del Perú* (Cordova, 1617), also played a role in this. Garcilaso, himself an Inca, described Incan customs and public ceremonies as if they represented an ideal (JJ).

76. The cruel treatment of madmen stemmed from the belief that they were possessed (MK).

77. During the Polish Enlightenment, *philosopher* could imply "social reformer" (MK).

78. Three verdicts received in abstentia meant forfeiture of protection under common law (MK).

79. Delegates to the Diet elected by dietines were provided with instructions from the gentry concerning stands on matters affecting both the country as a whole and the region represented. The delegates were supposed to abide by these instructions unquestioningly, *"etiam sub discrimine* the Diet" (even if doing so means breaking off the session) (JJ).

80. *Panis bene merentium,* "the bread of the worthy," crown lands set aside to reward those performing services for the common good and distributed by the king himself (JJ).

81. The litigious gentry attached great importance to these two city halls, since court sessions were held in them.

82. *Salus publica suprema lex esto,* "let the public good be the highest law" (actually, *salus res publicae,* "the good of the republic"). A famous and oft-cited principle of Roman law (MK).

83. *Pro primo et principali obiecto,* "as our first and principal goal."

84. "The matter of the Neapolitan sums and the opening of the Olkuszian mines" were traditional charges to Diets. The Poles continued their efforts to get the Spanish to repay the Neapolitan "sums" (430,000 ducats) lent by Polish queen Bona Sforza to King Philip II in the sixteenth century, and the matter was discussed again and again by the Diet. Similarly, there was repeated talk of solving Poland's financial woes by reopening the Olkusz lead and silver mines. The mines had been worked from the thirteenth to the sixteenth centuries. Some had been overmined, and others were destroyed during the Swedish invasion of Poland in the seventeenth century (JJ).

85. Faced with a huge increase in ecclesiastical lands resulting from bequests and endowments, a law was passed in the seventeenth century mandating approval by the Diet of any new endowment benefiting a cloister or the Church (MK).

86. *Caetera activitati,* "other matters."

87. For *"etiam sub discrimine* the Diet," see n. 79; *non ad destructionem, sed ad aedificationem,* "not to destroy, but to build."

88. *Zelum boni publici,* "fervor for the commonweal."